IN CHRIST
THERE IS
NO EAST
OR WEST

IN CHRIST THERE IS NO EAST OR WEST

Kent Nussey

Quarry Press

Several of these stories have been published previously, although in slightly different form. "In Christ There Is No East or West" appeared in *Black Warrior Review*, won the *Black Warrior* Annual Fiction Prize, 1986, and was anthologized in *The New Generation* (Doubleday); "Laughter of Young Women" appeared in *Crazy Horse*; "Crossing the Border" appeared in *Sequoia,* and the Kingston *Whig-Standard* Magazine; and "Perfect Figures" appeared in *Prism* (New York).

The author wishes to thank the Ontario Arts Council and The Creative Writing Center at Stanford University for the material encouragement and moral support that went into the making of this book.

The publisher gratefully acknowledges the financial assistance of The Canada Council and the Ontario Arts Council.

Canadian Cataloguing in Publication Data
Nussey, Kent
      In Christ there is no east or west
ISBN 1-55082-046-X
I. Title.
PS8577.U86I6 1992 C813'.54 C92-090448-3
PR9199.3.N88I6 1992

Cover art entitled *Freeways, 1978* by Wayne Thiebaud, reproduced by permission of the artist.
Design by Keith Abraham.
Typeset by Larry Harris.
Printed and bound in Canada by Best-Gagné, Toronto, Ontario.

Published by
Quarry Press, Inc.,
P.O. Box 1061, Kingston, Ontario K7L 4Y5.

*And the four Points are thus beheld in Great Eternity:
West, the Circumference; South, the Zenith; North, the
Nadir; East, the Center, unapproachable for ever.*

William Blake, *Jerusalem.*

for Julian and Maureen

CONTENTS

CROSSING THE BORDER

Still in Ontario, about forty kilometers from the border, Matthew's father started on the hymns. He sang the familiar ones, a few snatches of verse, replacing forgotten phrases with resonant "tro-doe-doe" riffs. And then the relentless chorus: "*For me . . . He died, for me . . . He lives, and everlasting light and life . . .*"

Matthew winced and held himself in check. They were driving down to Syracuse where Matthew's wife, Tina, lived. After six years of marriage, the last two spent on opposite coasts, they'd sign divorce papers this afternoon. Matthew squeezed his eyes shut against the sun firing on the little Buick's metallic burgundy hood. A lingering summer cold had gone into his ears. His father's voice changed tune. It seemed to filter through an ancient radio.

"*You ask me how I know He lives, He lives . . .*" his voice crescendoed and cracked, "*. . . within my heart!*"

Behind Matthew's eyes, against his sinuses, a tremendous vacuum ached. He steadied himself against the dash and blinked.

"Dad," he said. "I wonder if you could ease up for awhile."

His father glanced at him. "What's wrong?"

"My head. This cold. The heat."

He reached into his shirt pocket for the aspirin bottle and spilled two tablets into his palm. He tossed them back, gulped, grimaced.

"Don't let it get to you," his father said. "You'll live through this."

"Why should I? What's the point?" said Matthew.

Today was the culmination of a long torture. He'd been defeated, he believed, by Tina's friends and analysts, clear heads who'd convinced her that what Matthew called love was more nearly obsession. A disease to be routed. In their late night cross-country phone calls she'd talked about emotional health and independence. She told him that he had to find himself.

"It's hard, I know," his father said. He steered with his hands hooked loosely on the lower half of the wheel, knees akimbo. "I know what it's like when you want to quit. Thirty years ago, when the diabetes hit me, I thought I was finished. I had a small congregation and a young family. Big bills. Everyone wanted money. I had to talk to myself. I said, It won't always be like this."

The car swerved slightly and drifted back to the middle of the highway, straddling the broken white line. Matthew released a long, noisy breath. He wanted to remain calm this trip. Since he'd flown in from California last week he'd made too many caustic asides and vaguely blasphemous remarks.

His father said, "Think of all the times we've traveled this road since you were a kid. We've seen some awful weather. Beautiful autumns. How old are you?"

"Twenty-seven."

"Imagine. Hundreds of times up and down this highway, over the border. You could almost work it out mathematically."

Matthew stared out the window. Not yet ten o'clock and the sun blistered the black asphalt; the trees and bushes seemed to boil up green and angry.

"I wish it were over," he said. "I wish I were dead."

His father frowned. "Don't," he said. "Please, son. Go easy on yourself."

A massive transport roared by in a blast of pebbles and heat. His father started, as if he'd been slapped, and the car leaned toward the shoulder. For breathless seconds the right tires rode the pavement's edge. Matthew closed his eyes. The car swung lazily back to the middle of the road.

"Watch it."

"I'm watching it," his father said.

"You're all over the road. Let me drive."

"It'll be your turn on the other side. We'll switch after the border."

"I hate this. I hate it," Matthew said.

His father looked down the road.

"I have faith in you," he said. "And I have faith in God." He said this almost sadly, as if he were sorry, nonetheless, that faith was all they had.

Up ahead they saw the highway curve out of the trees, dip to the horizon's blue haze and reemerge in the sky, cat-cradled in the first of the great bridges spanning the Saint Lawrence.

"All right," Matthew said. "When we get to Customs don't say anything about lawyers or divorce. It'll only make them curious. Say we're visiting relatives."

His father sniffed. "They've never bothered me here. I've crossed hundreds of times and I've never had trouble."

"Just the same. We're visiting relatives."

The bridge lifted them high over the river, miles wide from bank to bank on the horizon. Matthew looked down at the islands and boats on the glittering slate. A Great Lakes tanker pushed upstream, a tiny wing of foam against the inexorable black hull. He recollected crossing this bridge with Tina, the particular thrill of coming down fast, out of the sun or stars like a spaceship, into a different country.

His father touched the brake as they leveled out in the trees and traffic. A sign with the governor's name on it said WELCOME TO NEW YORK, THE EMPIRE STATE.

"Remember,"Matthew said. "Just visiting."

His father nosed the Buick into a line of cars and RVs

waiting for inspection at one of the booths.

"The other line's moving faster," said Matthew.

"This is fine."

Matthew rolled the window and looked out. Heat swam up from the pavement.

"Look. They're zipping through the next booth. Look at that."

His father peered and clicked his tongue. He glanced in the rearview and swung out. Horns shrilled in the heavy air and Matthew looked over his shoulder. A woman in a blue pick-up gave him the finger. His father shook his head.

"It's going to be a hot one," he said.

The car in front pulled away and they eased into the shade, beside the uniformed man up on his stool in the booth. Matthew removed his sunglasses and folded his hands in his lap.

The man tapped some buttons on his computer and leaned out, squinting.

"Citizens of what country?" he asked.

Matthew's father licked his lips and considered, as if this simple question had thrown a new light on an old and troublesome dilemma.

"It's not so complicated as it seems," his father said. He jerked his head at Matthew. "He's American. I'm not."

The man squinted harder, his eyes hard creases.

"Purpose of visit?"

"Just over for the day," said his father, assuming a formal attitude.

"But for what purpose?"

Matthew's father rested his hands high on the wheel.

"We're coming back in the evening," he said.

"Where did you say you were from?"

His father motioned with his hand. "Back there," he said.

Matthew couldn't believe what he was hearing. He blinked at his father and the man. He opened and closed his mouth.

The man stepped out of his booth of steel and glass and squatted beside the car. He pushed his face close to Matthew's father and grinned unpleasantly.

"Okay, wait," the man said. "Here's what I'm asking you. I'm asking *why* you want to enter this country. Is this trip for business or pleasure?"

His father flexed his hands on the wheel. The moment he spoke he made eye-contact with the man.

"*You* might call it pleasure," he said.

Matthew leaned across his father, he nodded furiously.

"This is my father. He's my father!" he said. "He's retired. He's a minister. I'm American. We're just visiting our relations. Down and back today." He smiled and pumped his head up and down.

The man drew a breath and looked in the car at the steering column, the radio, the paper sack and the thermos on the seat behind them. He straightened and dropped his hand on the roof. They couldn't see his face.

He said, "Okay. Take off."

They pulled into the sunshine and climbed the ramp to the highway. Matthew rubbed the sweat from his eyes and loosened his seat-belt.

"Incredible," he said. "Just incredible."

"You made me nervous. Normally, I'm not like that."

"Right. I made you nervous." Then, despite himself, "God damn."

The car floated onto the long empty road and fixed itself to the broken yellow line. A different country. Green rising fields scabbed with tree stumps and sagging farm houses. Dead cars sprouting TV antennae. Matthew wished he were drunk. It was a longing he'd been unfamiliar with until this year, and lately the urge had become especially keen. Last week, his second night home, he'd been awakened by noises from the kitchen.

"Sit down. Stop talking and drink this," he heard his mother say, and he knew his father was having an insulin reaction, laughing and staggering like an inebriate. A choice irony, since his father claimed he hadn't tasted alcohol since he was eighteen. Matthew heard a chair fall over, then the front door swing open. He got out of bed and went down.

From the hallway his mother motioned. "He won't drink the juice," she said. "It's happening more often, lately. Look at him." Matthew felt the night air on the thin sweat of his neck and forehead. His father stood outside the screen door in his pajamas, his arms raised high.

"Praise God," his father said. "My soul magnifieth the Lord!"

"Dad," Matthew said, trying to draw him into the doorway. His father laughed and shook off his hand.

"God is good!" he cried.

Over his father's shoulder Matthew saw the dark shape of the car in the driveway, silent and fixed like a stone. The air was soft with the scents of flowers and watered lawns. Down the street a TV was on, serious cinematic voices against big band music and canned laughter. Suddenly, more than anything else, Matthew wanted a drink. He wanted to walk across to the little shopping plaza and sit in a cool suburban bar and drink cold beer and scotch.

Then his mother moved in with a tumbler of sweet pineapple juice and his father emptied it in hard, hungry swallows. In five minutes he was calm, sitting at the kitchen table, mopping his brow with a dish cloth. Matthew stepped outside in his shorts and sat on the stoop. He could hear his mother gently scold and his father apologize, until at last he heard nothing but the TV down the street.

On Route 81, no traffic. Matthew reached into the back for the thermos and held it between them.

"Want any of this?"

"I'm fine," his father said. "No thank you."

"Just a sip, to keep your edge?"

"I'm fine. Have some yourself."

Matthew poured the fruit punch into the thermos cup, looked at it, and poured it back. He capped the thermos with the cup and dropped it on the back seat.

"I'll wait," he said.

A truck roared out of the wind; the chrome-studded wheels flashed in Matthew's eyes. He groaned and squeezed the bridge of this nose.

"It's so hot," he said.

"Must get hotter than this in California."

"Yes, but it's different."

"Maybe it's the humidity," his father said.

Matthew watched his father's hands on the wheel. His fingers were slender and tentative, the nails ridged and clean. He wore no rings, not even a wedding band. A phrase, probably Biblical, came to mind: *The sweetness of his hands.* In the pulpit, when he raised his hands, his father seemed to draw a collective breath from his congregations. A pause, a silence of portent. In those moments Matthew saw his father clearly. He thought he'd seen his father as God saw him. He saw God's love on him. As a child he'd take his father's hand in his own and trace the lines and creases of the palm.

Sweet.

"This business with Tina," Matthew said. "It's not healthy."

His father nodded. "I understand. You'll come through."

"It never ends," Matthew said. "Will this end it?"

His father chewed an edge of his lower lip. He touched the window with his finger.

"Look at this country," he said. "You always loved this neck of the state. Sit back and enjoy it. Don't think about this afternoon."

Matthew shook his head and yanked the shoulder harness away from his chest.

"Why don't I drive now?"

"Watertown, maybe. Maybe I'll stop and make some calls in Watertown."

Before retiring to Ontario, his father had worked parishes throughout the state: Watertown, Syracuse, a handful of small churches in the Southern Tier. He regarded his fellow ministers from these times and places with an esteem that still surprised Matthew. Many of them were bombastic half-educated men. His father knew them as Tommy or Rupert or Bev or Alton, oddly romantic and antiquated names that Matthew associated with World War I or Oxford in the Twenties. To his father, they remained fellow foot soldiers in a great crusade.

"You and your phone calls," Matthew said. "You deserve better friends."

His father looked at him for a moment, as though he were a grief-stricken parishioner, someone gone abstract and out of himself with unhappiness. He turned his eyes back to the road and nodded. He said, "This is poor land. Poor, but there's character here. Back in Canada, I know the earth. I know where the roads go and I can tell by the clouds if it'll rain or snow. But down here I know people. When I'm gone they'll remember me here, not up north. Sometimes I wonder why I went back to Ontario."

Matthew felt that he was close to something real and final, something about his father, or himself, or the place they were seeing. He wanted to stop and hold onto it. He wanted to get out and walk into it and hold on.

"If I only knew it, then," his father said, cheerily. "But the facts are never in. You never get all the information."

"The very night she decided to give up on us, I knew," Matthew said. "We were a continent apart, but I could tell."

His father drove for a minute without speaking. Then he said, "Let's get the news." And he reached and switched on the radio.

Just after two they parked in front of Tina's building. They got out, looking up at the windows that might be hers, and went inside. At the second floor landing a door opened and she leaned out. She looked at Matthew's father and said, "This is a surprise." As they stepped through the door she turned to Matthew. "You look different," she said. "Heavier or something."

For a moment they stood there, surveying the potted plants and framed prints on the wall.

"This is pleasant," his father said. "I like this."

"I sanded the floors myself. What a job. Never again."

Matthew saw that she had succeeded in making a home without him.

"How about some iced tea?" she said. She moved deliberately and spoke clearly. She wore a loose wrap-around skirt and a sleeveless white jersey. To Matthew, she appeared ferociously calm.

His father asked for the bathroom to wash up. Tina pointed and he disappeared around a corner. They stood listening to the running water.

"How is he? Why did he come?"

"He says he wants to get in touch with some preacher friends. I think it had more to do with the car. He doesn't like the way I drive."

She shook her head. "He drove all the way? You shouldn't let him."

"It's his car. He has a thing about his cars."

"He should quit while he's ahead."

Matthew fished a handkerchief from his pocket and pretended to blow his nose.

"He's all right," he said. And then, "I need a stiff drink."

She looked into his eyes with a coolness and curiosity that was almost medical.

"Can you do this?" she said. She turned away. "We'll get a beer later, downtown. Now I'll get the tea."

In a few minutes she returned carrying a tray set with two full glasses, a small sugar bowl, and two spoons. She put the tray on a low table beside Matthew and sat across from him in a wide wicker chair. He shook a pill from the container in his pocket and chased it with cold tea. He understood that everything he did provided her with more evidence that she'd made the right decision.

His father stepped around the corner, smiling.

"You've done a nice job with this place," he said to Tina. "This is a nice apartment."

Matthew regarded the bookshelves and the aquarium; he lifted his feet, one after the other, to look at the oriental rug. The red diamond pattern seemed to pulsate, opening and closing.

"Let's get to work," he said. "Let's finish this."

They gave his father more tea and magazines and made him comfortable on the couch. Then they went outside to Tina's car and drove into town. The heat bore down with humidity and smog. Matthew struggled for breath while Tina drove.

"This is no fun for me, either," she said.

"I'll be okay as soon as we sign those papers."

She slowed before the traffic light and looked at him.

"I'd like to end this amicably," she said.

"We are. It is," he said.

But he knew he'd never be with her again.

By four-thirty they were back at the apartment. When Tina opened the door they heard his father speaking loudly into the telephone.

"They're in big trouble in Rochester," he said. "The Wesleyans don't know where the action is anymore." He looked up and waved at them. Another man might be talking to his bookie in the same voice, Matthew thought.

"Let's go, Dad."

His father nodded. Matthew could hear a tiny voice in the receiver.

"Dad, let's get out of here."

"All right," he said. "My son's here, Harold. I have to go. But give my regards to Marian and keep those Free Methodists honest. And hello to Doug."

He replaced the receiver, smiling.

"That was Harold Mack. He pastors the Free Methodists in Baldwinsville. They're putting the other denominations out of business down there."

His father chuckled and folded his hands.

"All right, let's get on the road," Matthew said.

Tina followed them to the parking lot. His father nodded at the sky and stared.

"Looks like a storm coming in from the north," he said. "Where are the keys?"

"I'm driving," Matthew said.

He swung himself behind the wheel, slammed the door, and snugged the seat-belt. In the rearview he watched his father say goodbye to Tina. They embraced and stepped back. Weeks from now, in California, he'd recollect this moment. He'd drink hard for a month and maybe by Christmas he'd be okay. Just now, the thing was to drive clear of this place.

He rolled down the window and thumped his fist against the warm metal.

"I'm coming," his father said.

As he came around the car Matthew saw him as strangers must have seen him: a graying gentleman in pressed slacks worn a tad too high, canvas shoes from the discount store and plaid socks, a face that was utterly trustworthy and trusting. The sort of older man you spot in the Post Office or grocery store, retired men who have worked hard and stayed married, teachers or solid businessmen, society's foundation. That entire generation. Where will we be when they're gone? Matthew asked himself. What will the world become?

"Here I am," his father said, closing the door lightly.

Turning out of the lot they both looked over their shoulders, and his father started to wave, but Tina had already disappeared.

On 81 again, going north, a flat gray lid closed on the sky. On either side of the highway, below the trees, the houses and fast food joints seemed held in a pressurized stasis, a vacuum between hot earth and solid cloud. Matthew swallowed to pop his ears and drove fast. His father produced a handful of jelly beans from his shirt pocket and ate them one by one from his open palm.

"Let me know when you're tired," he said.

"We just started. I'm fine."

"Okay. Any time."

Matthew glanced at him. "What about you?" he said,

eyeing the candy. "It's been a long day. What about those sandwiches Mom packed?"

"No, no, I can wait."

A siren started up behind them and Matthew saw the revolving blue and reds streak his rearview mirror. A moment later the police car screamed by in the passing lane. Half a mile down the road it exited, and then they saw the black smoke and ash rising against the gray sky. As they passed they craned to see the burning house, the red lights of the fire trucks throbbing on the flat air.

"Look at that," his father said. "Isn't that something?" He turned stiffly in the seat and stared at the shrinking pillar of smoke.

"It looks like something, doesn't it?"

Matthew blinked in the rearview. "What do you mean, like something?"

"All that black smoke standing in the sky. It looks like something alive."

"Like what? What does it look like?"

His father shrugged and smiled. "The thing is, as soon as they put it out the rain will start."

Matthew looked at his father.

"We'll pull over and eat soon," he said.

"You're hungry? You want a sandwich?"

Matthew didn't answer. He rolled the window all the way down and plunged his head into he thick rushing air. He gulped and steadied himself.

"Talk to me, Dad. Tell me something you've never told me before."

His father folded his hands loosely. "What would you like to hear?"

"Something new. Something that happened to you that I don't know about."

His father leaned back in the seat and began a story about his first parish, a church in a small upstate town called Buena Vista. He talked about the big cold house where he lived alone, how he lay awake nights listening to the rats in the attic. He mentioned how the water froze in the basin overnight, how he stoked the cook-stove until it glowed. It was winter and war-time: his friends and brothers were overseas. He was thirty-three and unmarried. It was not a new story. In fact, Matthew had heard many versions throughout his life. But he understood that there was an urgency and meaning behind this story which his father had never successfully communicated.

"I had the whole house to myself," his father said. "But I couldn't take it. I got out, rented a warm room in town. I didn't feel good about that, either. Seemed like a failure of faith."

Matthew closed his eyes and drove by touch, the feel of the road.

"It's one year I can't forget. Living alone in that old farm house while the news was full of Europe and Japan."

In the distance outside the car the world shuddered and rolled. Matthew opened his eyes.

"Thunder," said his father. "Here comes that rain."

Something was happening out there. Through his cold Matthew thought he could smell something oily and alive.

"It'll clear this heat. Your mother will worry, but a heavy rain is just what we need."

"What time is it?"

His father checked his watch and slid it off his wrist.

"Almost seven," he said. He laid the watch face up on his knee.

"It's later than seven," Matthew said.

"No, that's the light. This watch keeps time. It's seven."

Matthew reached down and snapped the radio on. For a few seconds they listened to the lightning crackle through the speaker.

"It's going to be a real storm," his father said.

They knew they were near the border when they spotted the picnic area, some painted tables on an island of grass nearly surrounded by trees. Matthew steered out of the right lane and exited slowly. The pavement banked and dropped into the maples and birches and pines. The little parking lot was empty.

"Let's just eat a sandwich and relax for five minutes."

"You're tired," his father said. "This has been rough on you. I can take us the rest of the way."

"All right. Maybe," Matthew said.

They rolled the windows up and got out. From moment to moment the sky darkened and leaned toward the earth. The tables, grass, and trees stood out in peculiar relief, as if in a light of their own.

They put the bag on a table but they didn't sit down. His father took out two sandwiches wrapped in waxed paper.

"Take this," he said, and he handed one to Matthew.

Matthew folded back the paper and bit in. He swallowed and listened to the highway noise above the trees. The sound of invisible traffic faded; he heard low thunder and the crumpling of waxed paper as they ate.

A bead of rain struck Matthew's face and he looked up, blinking.

"Here it comes," he said.

His father smiled, thoughtfully chewing.

The wind hissed softly in the branches. It rippled the uncut lawns. A foam cup tumbled by, popping, talking, spouting names. Matthew glanced back at the car. The crimson finish reflected a vibration from the sky, a darkening current. Cold rain fell on his face and hands.

"We better get in," he said, folding the paper over what remained of his sandwich.

His father nodded and turned his face toward the rainy murmur in the trees.

Matthew walked to the car, opened the door with his key, and got in. He leaned over to the driver's side, but it wasn't locked. The rain fell harder, drumming on the car and blurring the blacktop. He looked out at his father, who had not moved from picnic table.

Matthew cranked open the window a few inches. "Dad," he called. "Dad, get in."

Through the rain he heard the rush of a great wind. It moved toward them from over the highway, behind the trees. His father stood perfectly still with his head lifted as if to hear a secret voice. The rain bleared the windshield and blew inside. The car rocked slightly in the wind. Matthew closed the window; he planted both hands on the dashboard and waited for everything to stop. He waited for the other door to open, for his father to slide in beside him and say, Let's go home.

LAUGHTER OF YOUNG WOMEN

It hadn't been a good day for Bernie. He fell asleep in history class and woke to find he'd been assigned extra homework. Worse yet, Raeleen had to make up a biology lab and couldn't meet him for lunch. In the final study hall of the day some tenth graders threw tiny balls of clay at the back of his head. After school he stayed another hour for band practice. His pitch was consistently flat and the other french horns gave him dirty looks.

It was nearly five o'clock when he stepped into Smitty's Diner with his instrument case. His hands were wet and cold and his hair was plastered to his forehead with rain. Raeleen was working the counter. A row of squat men in dirty plaid jackets and billed caps watched her move back and forth with the steaming coffee pot in her hand. Their heads turned as Bernie took a stool at the end. His horn tumbled off the foot ledge and whammed against the floor. The men laughed.

"Lover boy's here," said a pie-faced man with a knuckle hooked through a coffee cup.

Bernie looked at the man. The man met his look.

"Leave him alone, Tom," Raeleen said. She refilled the man's cup and moved down the counter to Bernie.

"How was band?" she asked. She crossed her arms behind her back and went up on the balls of her feet as she spoke.

"Horrible. I hate the french horn and I missed my bus."

"You're in one of your moods."

"It's been that kind of day," he said. "When do you get off?"

"Seven, same as always. Can you stay?"

"Naw, Pobjoy socked me with a paper. I have to get home."

"Want a Coke?" she said, turning away.

"All right. No ice."

Bernie watched her stretch for the wax-paper cups. The short white dress inched up her thighs. Bernie glanced quickly at the row of men. They grinned at him.

"Here," said Raeleen, pushing the cup toward him.

In a low tense voice he said, "I hate this place."

She frowned at him. "You blow everything out of

proportion. Everything's a big deal with you."

"This place stinks."

"Look," she said, squaring her shoulders. "I'm not going to let you depress me again. It's a job."

She went to turn a meat paddy on the grill. It hissed and a plume of greasy smoke rose above her. The bad air was affecting his head, Bernie thought. He thought he felt a cold coming on.

On the highway he breathed easier, though the rain fell steady and cold. He considered what a dismal affair his life would be without Raeleen. And yet, he depressed her. She'd said it. He felt ashamed. But on the other hand, who wouldn't be depressed, living around here? His gaze took in the unturned fields, broken with outcroppings of rocks and black tree stumps. Brown pools had gathered in the low stretches near the highway. He walked with his head down, his chin tucked into the zipped collar of his nylon jacket. Two cars passed before he turned to show his thumb. In the distance the hills blurred behind a veil of low sky and rain.

The third car was a long fishtailed Pontiac with a toothy grill and round headlamps that glowed in the late afternoon. The car swooped toward him and Bernie shuddered slightly as it slowed and stopped on the gravel shoulder. He ran to it with the french horn case bumping his knee. The door on the passenger side swung open and Bernie ducked in, catching the case between his knees. He'd hardly shut the door before the car was moving again.

"Thanks," Bernie said, and he looked at the driver.

She was a young woman, maybe in her twenties, maybe older: in the first glimpse there was no telling. She smiled and accelerated. She wore a blue athletic jacket with a gold patch on the shoulder that said "Bulldogs." Her hair was a bad bleached yellow and her right hand, which held a cigarette away from the wheel, bore a short bluish scar between her thumb and first finger. Bernie wanted to stare at it but the hand moved jerkily between the steering wheel and the ashtray beneath the dash. Little gray ashes sat between the creases of her jeans.

"It's raining like a bitch," she said. "It rains ten months of the year in this fucking state. That's Sherry in back."

Bernie twisted around to nod at the girl behind him. She was younger than the driver, a skinny girl with thin black hair and shadows under her eyes. Her mouth twitched at him but she did not return his nod. Bernie watched the road in front of him.

The windshield was stained with a gray-blue film. The dash was littered with matchbooks that said "State Bank of Fillmore" and "King Edward Cigars."

"Where you headed?" asked the driver.

"Just down to Homer," said Bernie.

"Homer," she said. "That's a waste of a town. That's one nothing place to live. What do you say, Sherry?"

"Homer's a shit hole," said the voice in back. Bernie felt it on his neck, the uneasy air, as if someone were sharpening a straight razor on a strop behind him.

"What say to that?" the driver asked, and before Bernie could answer she said, "What'd you say your name was?"

Bernie took a breath. "Harold," he said.

"Harold," said the driver. "That's a good one."

The girl in back made a short sound. Bernie decided he wouldn't look around again.

"Harold," said the driver. "That's a waste of a name."

Bernie kept his eyes on the countryside, the dreary March harshness of the fields that had barely lost their snow, the grim and infrequent little houses behind sagging barns. Long stretches of brown weeds and mud.

"Hey, don't get us wrong," said the driver. "You smoke? You want a smoke?" She shook a pack of Lucky Strikes at him.

"I don't smoke," he said.

"Ha. That fits. A million guys with habits and I pick the one that don't smoke."

Sherry snorted at the back of his neck.

He felt dizzy. He closed his eyes and angled his thoughts toward Raeleen. There was fine summer afternoon when he'd happened to see her playing tennis with Tim Moler, captain of the baseball team. Raeleen's long, tan legs flashed in the sunlight as she rushed the net. In the middle of their set Bernie walked home and drove his brother's car to the abandoned quarry and cried and cried, bumping his head in a slow rhythm on the steering wheel.

"So Harold," the driver said. "you got a girlfriend?"

Bernie stiffened in the seat and faced her. "No," he said.

"Come on, Harold, what's that look? I bet you got a girlfriend back in Fillmore. Am I right?"

"I got girlfriends. So what?"

"What do they let you do?"

"What?"

"I said what do they let you do?"

The rain whipped against the windshield and the wipers squeaked softly, back and forth. Bernie made himself laugh, but he didn't answer.

"I mean, do you fuck these girls, or just kind of feel them up?"

Bernie shook his head and looked out the window. They were on the outskirts of his town. They passed the Keystone station and the trailer where Old Man Hardy lived.

"I bet he fucks them," the driver said. "What do you think Sherry?"

There was a pause and Bernie wondered if Sherry was laughing.

She said, "No, not this guy. He just kisses them. He's a kisser."

The driver laughed.

"I get off here," Bernie said. "I can get out right here."

She steered the long automobile down the main street of his town; Bernie watched Trombley's Town & Country Store and the Homer Inn float on the dingy windows and disappear as if the town were being sucked down a hole behind them.

"I have to get home," Bernie said. "My folks'll yell at me."

"What's the rush?" said the driver. "You got time for a ride."

"I have to get home," he said.

The driver cracked the window and pitched her cigarette. Bernie felt a tiny point of rain blow against his face before she rolled the window shut with a single hard twist. The girl behind him lit a fresh cigarette and expelled a fuggy cloud into the front seat. Bernie blinked and held his breath. He felt nauseous. His knees squeezed the instrument case.

"What's the matter, Harold? You don't look so good." The driver grinned and tugged her jeans at the crotch. "How about some music?" she said, and she switched on the radio. It crackled and sputtered and a nasal voice sang out of a great distance, "I got it bad and that ain't good . . ."

The driver fiddled with the tuning. She looked at Bernie.

"So Harold, what's your kind of music? I see you got some kind of instrument there. What do you play?"

Before he could answer she said, "What do you like on the radio?"

"Anything."

"How about your girlfriend? What does she like?"

Bernie opened his mouth and the voice behind him said, "I bet I know what she likes."

They laughed, beside and behind him, and the car swerved from the empty highway to a country road running up into the hills. The black bark on the trees shone like ebony and the gray saplings dripped silver rain. Soon it would be dark.

"Where are we going?" Bernie asked.

"You'll find out," the driver said.

The car continued uphill, the big engine laboring.

The road was mud and stones and the car lurched over deep ruts. Brown water streamed across the window on Bernie's side.

"This is it," said the voice behind him, and the driver swung the wheel. Bernie fell toward her and caught himself on the dash. The driver laughed and braked. They were in a weedy clearing surrounded by black pines. She killed the engine and gave Bernie a different kind of look. She wasn't smiling.

"You got a long walk home," she said.

Bernie clutched his horncase and threw the door open. He took three strides through the wet grass and then the one with the yellow hair moved in front of him and stood with one hand in her jeans and the other lifted as if to bring everything to a stop. The blue scar seemed to glow and squirm against her skin.

"Hold it," she said. "Behind you."

Bernie turned. The thin, dark girl stood beside the car with her hands on a length of steel or a crowbar or bumper-jack and it wasn't until she sighted him down the bore that Bernie realized it was a shotgun. He gripped the case. The rain fell against his mouth.

"Don't shoot," he said.

The blonde one said, "We got some questions for you, and don't try her. Sherry nails a buck every deer season. She likes to play with that thing."

Bernie's eyes stayed on the shotgun.

"Ask him something," said the thin girl.

"Okay, Harold. Let's see how smart you are. If you get two right answers in a row she may not shoot you where it hurts."

Bernie's knees wobbled. He held his free hand over his stomach as if to hide it.

"Question number one," the blonde one said. "Who's the best all-time singer in America?"

Bernie closed his eyes. He imagined Raeleen walking into the warmth of her well-lit house. He imagined her sitting in front of the television with a mug of Ovaltine in her hands, the sound of her mother's sewing machine in the next room.

The dark girl took two steps forward and jabbed him in the ribs with the snout of the gun. He gasped and half-buckled but he maintained his grip on the case.

"What about it?" she said.

"I don't know."

"Wrong," said the blonde one. "The answer is Elvis Presley." She stared at him with a pale, steady light on her face. "Question number two," she said. "Who's the second best singer of all-time?"

Bernie swallowed. "Male or female?"

She smiled. "Female," she said.

"Wait a minute. I can't think. Just give me a minute."

"Patsy Cline. You aren't real bright, are you Harold? Are you?"

"No," he said.

She said, "Here's your last chance. Get this one right and you're off the hook. You ready?"

Bernie nodded.

"Here it is. What's the best all-time American song?" The smile vanished again. "You better get this one right," she said.

His voice contracted in his throat and a small sound squeaked through his lips.

"*Duke of Earl*," the blonde one said. "Answer is *Duke of Earl*."

"You lose," said the skinny girl. She pointed the gun at his chest. The rain had soaked her hair flat around her face and behind her ears. The water ran down the black barrel and dripped from the end.

"Ask him something else," she said.

The other considered, grimacing. She said, "All right, I've got one. How old is your girlfriend, Harold?"

He heard her repeat the question and he heard himself say, "Seventeen. Same as me."

"What's her name?"

"Raeleen." The sound of his voice shamed him.

"Do you love her?"

They waited. Bernie listened to the rain drilling through the trees. He looked at their peaks silhouetted against the fading sky.

"Answer me," said the blonde one.

"I don't know," he said, and then in the same breath, taking a chance, he said, "Yes, I love her," and he thought he saw the thin girl wince.

The blonde one moved her tongue on her mouth. She said, "Good for you, Harold. Good for you." She moved behind the girl with the gun. "One last question," she said. "What's in the case?"

Bernie glanced down at it. "French horn," he said.

The girls laughed suddenly and loud, as if he'd betrayed the true colors of his soul.

The blonde one said, "I think I'd like to hear a song.

How about you, Sherry? Sherry and me want a song."

Bernie told himself that they only meant to frighten him, but the girl held the gun as if she'd used it before.

"Play something," she said.

"Take it out and play a tune."

"Take it out," said the girl with the gun.

Bernie kneeled and fumbled at the clips with numb fingers. He slid the cold mouthpiece into place and stood up with the horn. The pale coil glimmered in the rain.

"That's all there is to it," he said. "I can't play anything out here. I can't."

"Play us a song," said the girl with the gun.

"Play *Duke of Earl*," said the blonde one.

Bernie blinked at them. "I can't," he said.

The girl with the gun lowered it to her hip, level with his midsection. Bernie heard a click and her grip tightened.

"All right," Bernie said. "I'll try. But it won't sound like anything."

He snugged his fist into the bell. He drummed on the valves. Then he blew into the mouthpiece. His mouth was tight and dry.

"Play it," said the girl with the gun.

He took a deep breath and fit the small nickel cup to his lips. A few mournful notes blooped out and were swallowed in the rain and gathering darkness. He took another breath and stumbled into a tune, not any tune he'd heard before but something that came to his lungs and fingers from a part of him that was not scared.

"That's not it," said the blonde one.

Bernie faltered and started again, this time with a melody that might have been the one they wanted, as nearly as he could remember it. In flat hollow tones the recognizable rhythm rolled into the dark hills behind the rain. The girls did not move. Bernie closed his eyes and played the chorus again and again.

He heard the blonde girl say, "Good going, Harold. Keep playing."

"He heard their feet in the grass and sucking mud but he didn't look and he played the song until the engine roared and the high beams swept his face.

The salesman who stopped for him looked twice when Bernie climbed into the car.

"What's in the case?" the salesman said.

"French horn," said Bernie.

"You look cold. How about I give us some heat?"

Bernie didn't answer but the salesman pushed a switch and almost immediately a stale warmth filled the car. The salesman poured some coffee from a thermos with his free hand. He took a gulp and offered the plastic cup to Bernie.

As Bernie sipped the coffee, the salesman said, "I have a trunk full of vacuum cleaners. I don't suppose your mother's in the market for a good vacuum at a good price?"

Bernie didn't answer. The salesman shook his head.

"You'd think people didn't use them anymore," he said. "Nobody buys around here. I might as well go back to the city."

The heat blew on Bernie's face and hands and he felt the hot coffee working at the knot in his chest. He put his hand over his mouth as if he would laugh. He didn't laugh, he wasn't smiling, but he heard it in himself. Maybe it wasn't even his laughter, but it carried him down the road, a dozen years into the future, and he was with a woman who was not Raeleen, who sat beside him on a large rumpled bed, and he was telling the story about the girls in the Pontiac, how they'd made him play his horn in the rain. He laughed as he told it and the woman laughed and kissed the back of his neck and then he came back to himself trembling in the car, in the night, and he heard the salesman say, "Bud, you mind telling me what this is all about?"

PERFECT FIGURES

For days I'd been moving around my apartment like an amnesiac, smoking cigarettes near the telephone, mixing vodka and Gatorade at the feet of Freddette's statue. The eight foot papier mâché likeness of her that stood in my living room was a gift from early in our love. A self-portrait, like all her figures, this was the largest, like a giant praying mantis with arms uplifted in an abandonment of despair. The feet, long and narrow, were Freddette's feet. The small pointed breasts and thin, blade-like shoulders were definitely hers. The face registered a faint scowl, like someone trying to mask indigestion. I suspect she gave it to me because it failed to capture the intense vacancy of emotion she approached in the figures she called her best. All day her shadow loitered about my living room; at night the pale skin glowed like nuclear debris. I intended to saw her into pieces and stack them on the curb, but I couldn't do it. The figure was a survivor of the struggle between her nervous excesses and aesthetic ideas she developed the way other women work on particular muscles.

On Saturday afternoon I sat on the back porch with a beer, listening to the radio and reading the weekend magazine. The high school where I teach history had conducted commencement exercises a few days before and for the first time in months I felt off the hook. The sun was fine, the new grass shone green, and for a change Freddette was not in my thoughts. Looking for a good movie, I flipped to the cultural events calendar. An item under *Pick of The Week* caught my eye:

...he sat on a rock, naked save for a green necktie and a scar like a teensy smile on his ankle ...he looked like a talking seal and I was going to name him Benito, but instantly I recognized him as ROY ...I grabbed the tie and pulled him into the transition rites ...

Thus writes conceptual sculptor
Freddette Glass
about her upcoming
multi-media performance
ROY,
on the stage of the Artisera
Cooperative Gallery
next Wednesday night at 8:30.

This was set center page in italics and bold caps. I drank some beer and looked again. A multi-media performance called ROY. I'm called Roy. Roy is my name. For about a year Freddette and I had kept regular company. Then, as the good weather came on, she stopped phoning; she became difficult to locate. A month ago she suggested we take a break, not to see each other for awhile. How long? I asked. For as long as it takes, she said. Why? I asked. She said she had her reasons, as if it spoke volumes about me that I had to ask. No sweat, I said, and I went out and squandered a pay cheque on a mountain of Chinese food chased with a tidal wave of beer from the dingiest bars downtown.

Ms. Glass will appear on a minimalist set of three dimensional space to demonstrate her work in the New Objectivity. Audio assistance will come from rhythm specialist Robert Hummer and his Cosmo Drum Machine.

I went inside and dialed her number. A young man answered. "Freddette, please," I said. Into the distance he called her name. I heard her unmistakeable barefoot tread coming toward the phone. Freddette stumps along like her feet are made from wood, like the nerves are dead from the knees down. First time I saw her, on a day like this in early summer, she was walking her dog, a big setter with a flaming red coat the exact shade and texture as Freddette's fabulous hair. In fact, the dog looked like Freddette's hair come to life with tongue, teeth, and the same bewildered blue eyes. An absolute fluke, I'm told, in that breed. Freddette wore a black T-shirt from a pancake house and very dark glasses. Her foot was wrapped in an anvil of white bandage and she hobbled along on a bamboo cane like a war hero. For a moment, before we passed on the sidewalk, I thought she was blind. As they went by, the dog shot me a look of idiot woe; I had to stop and stare after them, at the gawky girl's body bound to the heavily plastered foot, the sun pouring syrupy glory on the tangle of hair against her black shirt and the dog, like a living four-footed wig of the same.

Later, after we'd spent time together, she admitted the cast was fraudulent, an art experiment, but there was no denying her actual clumsiness, her habit of slamming car doors on her digits or stepping in front of swooping bicyclists. When I mentioned these seemingly self-willed calamities she'd bristle and stare, or blatantly change the subject, like a soap opera actress.

I heard the receiver change hands, and then Freddette said, "This is Freddette."

"Freddette, this is Roy."

"Roy," she said.

"Yes, we have to talk. I'm looking at this thing in the paper about your show at the gallery. I want to know what's going on."

"The paper spells it out clearly, Roy."

"You know what I mean," I said. "What's this Roy stuff."

"There you go," she said. "Strictly paranoid."

"What about the green tie? And the scar. You can't say the scar is a coincidence."

"Listen, Roy," she said. "I can't talk now, but I don't

want your feelings hurt. Why don't you come to Jeff and Celia's place on Friday night. They're having a party. They won't mind an extra body, I'm sure. We'll talk then."

I hesitated. "Those people make me nervous," I said.

"That's not my fault. If you want to talk, come on Friday. It's the best I can do."

Freddette hung up and I took my beer into the living room. I sat on the sofa beneath her statue. I remembered the first time she showed me her studio in the old Continental Can building down near the bus station. When the Can people cleared out they sold it to the university press; when the press moved it was made into studios and rented to artists and dancers. We went at midnight and the building felt empty as Freddette led me through the dark echoing corridors and up two flights of stairs, each landing lit by a single red bulb. It took three different keys to unlock the door to her studio, and she relocked all three after we'd stepped inside. The big overhead fluorescents winked on, revealing a vast white room crowded with figures, at least a hundred papier mâché people, every one of them Freddette. They stood along the walls and faced center toward her work area as if waiting for another to be added to their number.

"All I have to do is produce the good one, the perfect figure," she said. "Mando Hawkes came through on his way to London. He said he'd show me at his place if I gave him the right one."

"What does he want?"

"The ideal vacuum. The complete non-statement. The figure that won't compromise itself with narrative implications. The figure that tells no stories."

I looked around the room. "Will that be difficult?" I asked.

She turned and glared at me. She said, "Roy, sometimes you make me think of corny old songs and dead pets."

I laughed it off, then. Later on, when I was driving around town and I saw her beautiful half-witted dog leashed to a parking meter or bike rack, I swear, I wanted to shove him into the trunk and drive off a bridge.

In the beginning, we spent considerable time in that studio, Freddette and me and the dog. I'd stop by after school with take-out food, which Freddette ate as she worked. Occasionally she'd ask the dog if he wanted me to walk him. His tail would drop and he'd raise the tragic blues of his eyes. "Guess not," Freddette would say, without turning from her work. When it was going well she'd take off her clothes, saying she needed to get naked with her materials. At first, for me, this was a natural turn-on. I'd light a cigarette and circle her until I came close enough to nudge her shoulder, to see how the plaster and powder made her tiny breasts look like clever imitations, and how the red of her hair shone in flagrant contrast like a house burning against thick fog. As I raised my hand Freddette looked me in the eye, and what she saw registered so plainly that I shrugged and retreated to the corner.

"It's nothing personal," she said. And that was the truth.

I told myself she'd been living too long on grants and commissions. She'd been away from the workaday world until she'd forgotten what people were, what they needed, and by people I mean her, Freddette, as much as myself. I resolved that I was good for her, that I kept her in touch with the rudiments, and eventually she'd know it. In the meantime, I'd maintain a positive attitude about her work.

Freddette's friends Celia and Jeff live on the second floor of an old frame house in the university area. Every month they throw a theme party where everyone wears make-up and esoteric clothing. Jeff and Celia never miss an opportunity to announce that their next-door neighbor is George Boyle, the poet. Published authors, no less poets, are not common in this town and although they hardly know him Celia and Jeff cherish the idea of George Boyle, as if he were an exotic tree that grew beside their house and nowhere else in the world. Last year, Freddette and I came to these parties regularly; I'd heard dozens of George Boyle stories, but I'd never seen the man. His house was usually dark, ghostly shades drawn over unlit windows. "He travels a lot," is Jeff's standard conclusion to a George Boyle story.

As I climbed the stairs to their flat on Friday night I heard excited voices talking about the poet. Earlier in the evening he'd come over to ask Celia to move her car.

When she saw me, Celia said, "It's true. We spoke. He said my car was blocking his driveway, just a little. He was afraid he'd scratch it backing out. What a dear. A real nice man." Then she said, "Roy!" as though she'd just recognized me.

"Freddette's supposed to meet me."

"Oh," she said, "isn't this great?" She waved her hand at the crowd. "Meg brought her videos and Robert's coming later with his tapes. We wanted to give Freddette a pre-performance party, to get her ready."

"Performance," I said.

"Next week at the gallery. You'll be there, won't you?"

"For sure."

Celia excused herself and I made my way toward the keg in the corner of the room. As I filled a plastic cup I noticed the television set suspended high in the opposite corner, a blue image that flickered down from the ceiling. I looked at it for a full minute before I recognized Freddette on the screen. She sat on a bench, staring. Now and then a bolt of static rippled the screen like the blink of an eye. The real Freddette hadn't arrived. I sidled over to the window for a look at George Boyle's house. Sure enough, he was home. A yellow light showed beneath a partly drawn shade in an upstairs room. I could see some hardwood floor and a littered desk.

"He'll never show," said a voice at my shoulder. Ron Childs peered over me to George Boyle's house. He held a pint of Four Roses to his chest. "You'll never see the great man," Ron said. "He knows when we're watching. On party nights he stays out of sight."

He drank from the bottle and shifted his stare to me. Ron tracks me down at these affairs because Freddette came to me directly from him last year. She left him with a suddenness that alarmed even me. Ron was a college quarterback turned thespian who landed the Marlon Brando and James Dean roles in the theater hereabouts. Now and then he appeared in a music video or modelled leather pants in the malls. He had the look. "Tragically muscled," Freddette called him. Tonight he wore tight black jeans and a sleeveless yellow jersey with red lettering that said, "Rimbaud Prayed For Death."

"Have you seen her?" I asked. "Freddette's supposed to meet me here."

A tight grin fixed itself to Ron's stony jaw.

"I should have known," he said. "I should have guessed."

He took another hit from the bottle. I thought it was just theatric drinking, but then he squeezed my arm and brought his face close to mine. He said, "You're not suffering, are you, Roy? You're not letting it get to you, I hope."

Up in the ceiling corner Freddette sat unmoved, unmoving in the grainy blue light. Ron let go and maneuvered into the other room. I stood there, massaging my arm until someone said my name.

"Over here, Roy."

It was Arlene Powell, the woman who does art reviews for the newspaper. In fact, Arlene had written the ROY piece. She smiled and nodded me over. Her sunburned face made her teeth look white and cool as vanilla ice cream.

"Roy," she said. "Where's Freddette?"

"You tell me."

"Oh, she'll turn up. We had lunch in her studio on Monday. She's pretty excited about this show. She thinks

Mando Hawkes might be there."

She talked on about Freddette and her figures in a friendly, neutral way. I liked Arlene for being older and calm, down-to-earth and earthy; the sweep of silver-gray in her hair gave her authority. Freddette had second thoughts about her. She said, "Arlene has an Anglo Saxon mean streak in her that doesn't know it exists." But I suspected she was mistaking critical candor for malicious intent.

"Arlene," I said. "What's going on? Something's going on with Freddette and I'm the only one who doesn't know."

She regarded me soberly, drink in hand.

"It's her work, Roy. Her work drives her to extremes. You have to appreciate that."

I do," I said. "I appreciate it." I turned to refill my cup and Arlene pressed her hand to my arm, exactly where Ron Childs had squeezed it.

She said, "It's just stuff, Roy. Forget about it. It's just stuff."

At midnight exactly Freddette appeared with Robert Hummer, the musician. He wore a long black trench coat and dark glasses, his hair pulled back in a ponytail that tightened the post-literate softness of his face. Freddette wore an oversized cardigan, her spectacular hair piled carelessly atop her head like something between burnoose and Davy Crockett cap. She refused to let her eyes meet mine. Hummer hunched into the room and raised a cassette tape over his head.

"She'll be in the stores next month," he said.

A long and religious "Ahh!" swept the party, followed by a general movement toward the pair. I smoked a cigarette in the corner beneath the TV until I caught her backing away from Jeff, the over-solicitous host.

"We have to talk," I said, steering her around by the elbow.

Her orange eyebrows knotted and her jaw clenched.

"Hello Roy," she said flatly. "Yes, we should talk."

"I want to know about this performance. Why my name? What are you trying to do to me?"

"I can understand your feelings," she said.

"Don't," I said. "Don't do it."

An emaciated Modigliani woman in a plaid jumpsuit snaked her arm around Freddette's waist.

"Fred honey," she said. "You must be climbing the walls. I want to hear all about it."

They drifted toward Hummer with the others.

I checked my watch and went back to the window that faced George Boyle's house. I took a breath and pressed my forehead to the cool pane glass. Across the darkness, a motion in the square of muffled light caught my eye. Over in the poet's house, behind the partly drawn shade, someone was standing. Visible from the chest down, he wore a western style shirt with pearl buttons and his stomach bulged slightly against the papers on his desk. I looked around, I wanted to tell someone, but the party had focused in the other room where Hummer's tape blasted away like rocket launch and machine-guns. People cheered. The dancing had begun.

Across the way George Boyle moved about his room, stopping to jog papers on the desktop, arranging them with his large, awkward-looking hands, making sure every-thing was right. Then he stepped out of view. Before the light went out, I saw the sheaf of manuscript on his desk, the clean ashtray, the orderliness of his craft. The room went dark and I was looking at the imperfect reflection of my face.

Freddette and Robert Hummer were dancing their own dance. Hummer spun in his flapping coat like a man reaching for a concealed weapon. Freddette's movement was minimal, small twitches and jerks. She looked like she did when she worked — spookily removed, almost inert. Hummer seemed physically stimulated by this; the less Freddette reacted, the more he whirled and spun. Ron Childs stood at the floor's edge, taking slugs from his bottle, watching everything.

The music stopped and Freddette made toward the kitchen. I acted quickly.

"What is it?" she said. "What now?"

A pale dampness gleamed on her neck and brow, but she wasn't the least breathless.

"You said we'd talk."

"I thought we had."

"I want to talk about your statues."

"Statues," she said, grimacing. "That's just it. That's just the problem. They are not statues, Roy. If you knew more about me and my work you wouldn't use that word."

"I know you," I said. "I know what you're doing with the statues, too. Instead of making them like you, you're trying to make yourself like them. You've got it backward."

"You're drunk," she said. "You're out of your depth."

"You couldn't make your statues tell a story if you wanted to."

"Go away, Roy. Nobody's listening."

"You don't know how to do it," I said. "You're good at something, but that isn't it."

Her face went white around deadly blue eyes. Her voice was high and weird. "Why do you always say the wrong thing?" she said. "Why do you always say the thing that makes it impossible to go on?"

I looked at the Freddette on the ceiling. I said, "I don't know. I can't help it."

She broke away and disappeared into the kitchen. Ron Childs came out of the yammering shadows and stood in front of me. He tapped my chest with the nearly empty bottle.

"You made her angry," he said. "You made Freddette angry."

"She's using my name. I have a right."

"Nobody makes Freddette angry. You make her angry and you've lost her. She's gone. I knew her a long time, and I never made her angry."

The cordy muscles stood out in his arm wrist and I expected the bottle in his grip to shatter in the next instant.

The last time I saw Freddette she was pacing on the stage of the Artisera Gallery wearing a paisley wet suit and an underwater mask. Her mouth was distorted around a black snorkel. The set itself was a three-sided room — two walls and a ceiling — painted robin's egg blue. It was just Freddette, the sound of gurgling water, and a single papier mâché figure — a smallish man with his arms folded and his face downcast as if he were trying to make a difficult decision or hold his temper. For ten, fifteen minutes she circled the figure, her flippers smacking the boards. I felt odd, sitting there in the dark, watching Freddette in her rubber suit and the increasingly familiar man in his stance of ill-humored defeat. I knew we weren't supposed to see her as Freddette, but now and then she'd look out at us through the V-shaped mask and all I could think of was her dog, the idiot setter, tied to a weight it couldn't budge.

She circled the plaster figure until the music started, the same music we'd heard at the party, and a strange medieval-looking instrument descended from the upper dark on invisible wires. Freddette lifted her arms and slowly, gently, the object slid into her hands. A nervous snicker ran through the audience. She was aiming a spear-gun at the papier mâché man. The music mounted to a scream like jets laying napalm over the desert; we clapped our hands over our ears just as Freddette fired a short, blunt spear through the man's chest. I jumped in my seat. The music stopped. Another trickle of laughter ran through the darkness. Freddette stared at us through her mask. The speared man stood his ground, his expression unchanged, except now he seemed to brood on the pro-jectile lodged in his chest rather than an abstract grief. The laughter caught on, followed by scattered applause.

I closed my eyes until the lights came up.

When the auditorium was more or less cleared, I lagged out behind the others. From his seat on the aisle

Ron Childs stood up and stepped in front of me.

"What is it?" I said. "What do you want?"

He stood there, working his jaw.

"Leave me alone, Ron."

Still, he didn't move. I thought that if I took my eyes off his, even for a second, something would happen.

Then he said, "She had to do it because of you. You ruined her for the rest of us."

Behind him, up near the exit, Arlene Powell was waiting. She called my name and Ron's eyes shifted. I moved around him and climbed the aisle to Arlene. She touched my shoulder and asked me what I thought of the performance.

I looked at her. "I'm not sure. What did you think? What will you write about it?"

Arlene shrugged and brushed her hand at the question.

"Oh well," she said. "Between us, the figure got the better of her. Freddette tripped up and told a story. Worse yet, she told a funny story."

I think I knew what Arlene was talking about. I think I understood what she was saying about the speared man on the stage.

As we moved through the lobby, she said, "Don't worry. Fred's too smart and ambitious to let this throw her. It's just a phase. Where'd you park?"

"Walked," I said.

Her jaw dropped. "In this neigborhood? That's insanity. Come on, I'll give you a lift."

Her little green Chevrolet was the last car in the lot behind the gallery. She took the long way to my place, swinging around downtown blocks deserted beneath orange lights that seemed to meld with the setting sun. She drove with the window open, shifting gears easily, her hands relaxed and in control. I recalled Freddette saying how Arlene was not what she seemed. Words to that effect. The sound of Arlene's voice and the car's motor had nothing to do with Freddette or her art, or our time together, and I could see how Freddette and Arlene were different and how they needed each other, although Arlene, as she drove, didn't seem to need a thing.

I rested my head on the seatback and watched her hands on the wheel.

We parked under the big trees that grew up around the streetlamp, the upper limbs tangled with soft, wet light. Arlene turned the engine off and we sat there.

"Go easy on her," I said.

"Don't worry," she said. She said it in the tone of general admonition, simple advice that could change everything.

I looked at Arlene and at the trees rising from the warm darkness and I thought about George Boyle, living alone in that house. I pictured him working through the night at his desk, capping his pens, holding his manuscripts. I saw his fingers spreading on the pages, almost tenderly, as if he were in love with his own life.

IN THE PICTURE

The last time I spent the night at my girlfriend's mother's house was just before Labor Day, in the middle of a heavy and depressing heat wave. I'd hardly been out of the apartment all week, sweating over my new strip, "Alfred the Beagle." My current one, "Oscar and Lance," was dying in the local paper. Alfred was the only idea I'd had in months, and his debut had to be perfect.

I was brainstorming grumpily, trying to sketch the first sequences, when Melba's mother called. Maybe I wasn't exactly pleasant on the phone. Mrs. Marcroft suggested I bring the work over to her place, since her husband was out of town and she'd as soon have the company. She said a new space might have a salutary effect on the drawing. It made sense. My apartment is hot and small. Besides, Melba would appreciate the gesture.

I told Mrs. Marcroft that Melba had taken my car to the city for the weekend. Fine, she said, she'd pick me up in front of my building at eight.

As her little station wagon pulled over I could see her laughing behind the wheel. She was still smiling from ear to ear when I climbed in with my drawing materials. I leaned across the leather seat and gave her a peck on the cheek. She smelled of sweet powder and hairspray.

"God, this neighborhood is dark!" she said, smiling. The car shot forward.

"This isn't a neighborhood."

She laughed. "I'll bet," she said.

Mrs. M looks like a president's wife. A First Lady. She's cheery and smart, she doesn't ask questions. The sort of comely silver-haired woman who keeps a tiny screwdriver at the bottom of her purse. Practical, but she's got her own ideas.

As we drove across town, out of the swimming heat between news stands and liquor stores, into the cooling suburbs, she laughed and talked about her night class.

"It's full of characters," she said. "The teacher is a riot. He makes droll remarks. The clothes he wears are about ten years out of date. Anyhow, he's plenty smart."

This class, which had begun the week before, would teach her how to program her personal computer for more efficient housework. The last course, a month back, explained techniques for making her mind more receptive to creativity. Melba and her mother share certain interests. They exchange books on Eastern thought and holistic medicine. They wear identical crystal pendants. A few weeks ago they spent an afternoon with a woman who paints "spiritual figures" in buttermilk. Melba says all this is strictly recreational, but I admit it worried me when her mother took her to a palm reader last winter when we were having trouble.

"I wish Alan could meet some of the people in this class," Mrs. M said. "He balks, every time. He thinks I'm introducing him to crazies. I keep telling him, it's computers, for heaven's sakes!"

Alan, her husband, Melba's father, is a mystery. In the ten months I've been seeing Melba I've never laid eyes on the man, not even in pictures. Melba says he looks like Perry Mason and speaks like Paul Harvey. He started in logging camps and now he nearly owns an oil company.

"I suppose Mr. Marcroft has a lot on his mind," I said.

Mrs. M gave me a swift glance.

"And what about Melba?" she said. She swerved to miss a VW coming out of a 7-Eleven. I saw the driver's face, a young woman, palely staring in the sweep of our lights.

"What about her?" I said.

"What about last summer when she was thinking of acting school? Why didn't her father encourage her a little? He didn't even ask her about it, never a word on the subject. He thinks everything but business is voodoo, or something."

I didn't know about that, one way or another, but I had a feeling for this man. He hadn't a clue that I spent these nights in his house. Mrs. M says he'd laugh at her for being uneasy alone, and Melba says he doesn't want to hear anything but good news. Still, he has a right. I told Melba. A man doesn't like to find things out later. Forget the money. He's fighting his own demons in the city, on the road, in his office in the back of the house. Money's just a color he works in, a medium in which he excels.

Mrs. Marcroft touched my knee with her finger.

"Changing the subject," she said. "Did Melba call you from work?"

"No, but Monday she said she had auditions until the weekend."

Mrs. M gave me another glance, more surprised this time.

"Why?" I said.

"What?" she said. "Oh, Bruce, I meant to tell you. My teacher is coming for coffee tomorrow. You ought to meet him. He's a riot."

She laughed and slapped the steering column. The horn squirted a short peal.

"I need to be back at my place early," I said.

She smiled and shook her head, what to make of a grown man who lost sleep over cartoon dogs. But I needed Alfred. Not merely to clear this career hump, but to get back my concentration. To get on track. He's a dog with a message, not just for kids and old folks, but a sign of the times. A beagle for the apocalypse.

"Well," said Mrs. M, "don't let it turn you into a drudge."

She turned onto the private road that wound through the dark trees and around the low houses snugged back behind gates, fences and shrubs. After a mile or so she turned again, sharply, and braked in the driveway.

"I'll be," she said. "Daren's here."

The other car sat like a shiny black egg outside the double garage. I got out and Mrs. M parked the station wagon inside. Daren's car ticked faintly, heat coming off the metal. Straight overhead, above the bushes and trees, the night-blue sky held a particular silence. Cool. Regular stars. We had a different sky over my building.

From the garage, Mrs. M called, "Let's find her."

I gathered up my drawing board and the old tackle box crammed with pens and pencils and met Mrs. M by the front door. She worked the key in the slot and dashed in to punch the code on the alarm. The house was wired tighter than the Russian embassy, windows that screamed if you breathed on them, stretches of carpet that fairly bristled at a glance. All that, and still she needed company. Or maybe because of it. I stepped carefully in this house. I looked at the floors and made myself think before I put my feet down.

"Daren must have turned it off," she said. "Come on. Are you hungry? There's beer and meat in the fridge."

She led me to the kitchen. Lights were on and somewhere in the house a radio played. She opened the refrigerator and whisked out cold cuts and a six pack. I spotted a book on the counter and flipped through it while Mrs. M made sandwiches.

"You ought to read that, Bruce," she said. "It'd teach you how to relax and use your talents more effectively."

"I don't need talent. I need a miracle."

She nodded and pushed a triple-decker of lettuce and turkey-baloney across the table. "I'm going to find Daren," she said.

She disappeared around the corner and I spread some mustard on the bread. Pushing the sandwich into my mouth, I wandered toward the laundry room, thinking I'd check the big freezer there for ice-cream bars. The back door was open. I rested my hand on the latch and looked out. An angle of light from behind me fell on the patio. Then heavy darkness, dim rustlings, sweet cool. I couldn't see the garden or the apple trees or the water, but the air was thick with their smells. I stepped from the light, toward the pool. The cover was off, the concrete ledges softly glowed, warm and chalky. And then the glow shaped itself into arms and legs, a woman's face, and though I saw her first the sandwich jumped from my hand when she spoke.

"You could drown," she said, sitting on the edge.

White bread, turkey, sliced pickle hit the water in little splashes.

"Hey," Daren said, "You're gunking up our pool."

She bent to scoop out the food. I looked down at the pale curves of her shoulder and thigh, the white blonde of her hair. She straightened and thrust the mushy bread into my hand.

"Take care of this," she said. "I'm getting back in."

"You startled me," I said. She was a lawyer in the city, and I'd never seen her in anything but business suits.

"What are you up to, prowling around out here, anyway? Where's Mom?"

"She brought me over. I think Melba wanted me to stay."

"I see," she said. I knew she was grinning. I looked at the water and thought about a swim, but she didn't ask me.

"I better get to work," I said. "Got a new strip on the boards."

She laughed, a laugh like her mother's and Melba's. A sound that got to me, never sure if they were laughing with or at, but nevertheless, a sound I craved.

"What is it this time?" she said. "Melba mentioned beagles. You're not doing beagles, are you?"

I heard something in the grass and turned to look. "That's right," I said, nodding, still looking over my shoulder.

"Bruce, beagles have been done, and by genius."

"This one'll be different. This one will say something."

I could see her eyes crease with amusement, I could see the silvery streaks of hair around her face.

She said, "Some people in my office were talking about the last one, the sea slugs."

"Oscar and Lance," I said.

"Yes, they seemed to think the social commentary was killing the visuals. I mean, they noticed you could draw, but — you don't have to be Cezanne or Picasso to produce a good comic strip."

"Right."

"Well, they had a point. Cartoons should be funny, after all."

She drew a sharp breath and swung her legs into the

water. The pool lights weren't on and there was no telling where the ripe dark left off and the deep water began. Same element. All night.

"There's funny and there's funny," I said.

"All right, don't get sensitive. You're so sensitive."

She lowered herself and pushed out into the water. For a moment there, talking to her voice, I had thought it was Melba or her mother telling me not to get sensitive. Melba or her mother, and the other two were behind us, hidden, listening.

Out in the starry water she turned on her back and raised her leg, a blade of soft light rising and falling, splash.

I went inside and tossed the sandwich into the disposal. Mrs. M was halving oranges with a knife as big as a machete.

"I'm in the mood for juice. You found Daren?"

"In the pool," I said.

"I thought I heard her talking. Do you think she'd like something to drink?"

I picked up my drawing tools. "You could ask her," I said.

Mrs. M regarded the window facing the back yard. That was her eldest daughter, her first-born, swimming out there in the dark.

"I have to get started," I said, but instead of heading toward the den I turned down the hallway.

The door to Daren's room was open. I looked in. Her clothes lay on the bed. Blouse, bright scarf, a pleated skirt. Stockings like deflated mauve legs dangled to the floor. Black slip on the chair. The room smelled vaguely of orchids. I noticed her high school photograph in a gold frame on the dresser. Same eyes, different hair; a sinuous black coil on her shoulder, the combed end touching her breast-bone. The mouth, full and red, obviously enhanced by the photographer's brush. The face in the picture was a variation on Melba's and their mother's, and as I considered it I wondered which face of the three most contained or contained more of whatever made Melba Melba. Or Daren Daren. Of the three women, who had more of it?

Somewhere a door slammed, and I took my work things back to the den on the far side of the house.

The coffee table in front of the couch was strewn with magazines. There were news weeklies and business periodicals, government reports, mail order catalogues from Maine and Wisconsin and New Zealand. One featured video recorders, thermal sox, and even a high tech crossbow, all on the same page.

Each magazine bore Mr. Marcroft's name on a little white label. In fact, his name was everywhere in this part of the house. The walls were hung with plaques and citations. The ceramic mugs on the mantel included his name in gothic script beneath the logo of his university.

Though I'd never seen him, I felt pretty sure I'd know Melba's father if I met him in a bar or on the street.

I made space for my drawing board and started.

After an hour, I pushed my work away and pinched the bridge of my nose. From the living room, behind the closed door, I heard women's voices. Not exactly an argument, but the talk had an edge. I heard Daren. Then I heard Mrs. M's voice, high and clear. "Well, why not?

Why shouldn't he?" she said. Daren answered in controlled tones, as though explaining to a child. "But why *not?*" her mother said.

Then the telephone rang. Phones rang all over the house. Mrs. M answered in the hall. I heard her say Melba's name and she laughed. I held the pencil between my teeth.

"Harry!" she said. "How on earth are you? Yes, she'll be tickled to death. Daren's here."

Daren said, "So how was Spain? Did you find the hotel? You dog. No, she's not. I'll tell her."

I couldn't make out the rest.

I found the remote control wand on the coffee table and pointed it at the television, a big Japanese model. The screen filled with aquamarine light and an astronaut appeared, floating in blue darkness. A thin cable hooked to his suit kept him from drifting away. His arms and legs moved slowly, like in bad dreams. Behind his helmet his eyes widened and closed, as if the immensity of space were too much for him. The volume was all the way down. I left it like that.

Around ten Mrs. Marcroft crept in, smiling and blinking, and asked if she was disturbing my work.

"It's not going to happen. Not tonight," I said. "I might as well turn in."

She bit her lip and touched my shoulder.

"I feel awful," she said. "Bringing you out here for nothing. I had no idea Daren was around."

"That's always the way," I said. I tried to keep myself from looking at the paper on my drawing board.

"Bruce, can I ask you something?"

I nodded.

"It's about Melba. I know I shouldn't burden you with a mother's concerns, but you know her so well."

"Thank you," I said, and wondered what I meant.

She dropped into the striped armchair across from me and flipped through a magazine.

"We get pounds of mail, every day, and it's all for Alan," she said. "He'll go for days without being in this house long enough to eat a meal, but he reads every piece of fourth class mail as if he's afraid he'll miss something."

"Melba," I said, "you said something about Melba."

She returned the magazine to the pile and looked at me. "I'm concerned about her happiness," she said. "She's hard on herself. You know. She pushes. Some people don't know how to be happy."

"She seems to know as well as any of us," I said.

"I wonder. She's so devoted to her friends. She gives so much. I'm afraid someone will take advantage."

I looked at my palms. I closed them on my knees.

"Of course," she said, "that's not all of it. There are complicating factors."

"I don't know all the people she knows," I said.

She looked at me, blinking. "No, she has a life that none of us are part of," she said, "and I don't know why I brought it up. But I trust you. You're a good influence on her."

We looked at each other. The way she looked at me made me wonder what she was seeing. Then, for some reason, we both looked at the TV. The space walker was still out there. Only this time his cable was gone; he tumbled and turned away from his ship. I lifted the remote control and hit the volume. The astronaut had quit struggling, and as the spacesuit shrank steadily into the void we heard the man inside saying the Lord's prayer.

I pushed a button and the picture blew up and rushed away. For a long moment we stared at the point of dying light. Mrs. M stood up, smoothing her lap. She touched my shoulder.

"Bruce, you're one in a million," she said.

I started to thank her again and caught myself.

When she was gone I picked up the pencil and put it back down. My heart beat slowly and I heard myself breathe, in and out. Alfred, my beagle, was far away. In someone else's imagination. Making tracks on a stranger's sketch pad.

The door opened once more and Daren leaned in. She wore a black robe with red piping on the cuffs and lapels, a man's robe. The cloth looked shiny, black as tar.

"Mom said you were watching TV," she said. "What's on?"

"Nothing's on."

"I was going to practice," she said.

"All right," I said.

"Practice my voice exercises. My scales. With the piano. Mom said you wouldn't mind."

I looked at the few lines I'd made on paper. I flexed my fingers and closed my eyes. When I opened them Daren was still there.

"Go ahead," I told her. "I'm done."

Her smile tightened into a look of professional concern.

"Why don't you get another sandwich?" she said. "Or a beer."

She closed the door behind her and started in on the piano. I sat on the couch and looked at my hands, my pencils. In the other room Daren's voice rose and fell and stretched single notes. I switched off the lights and went out. Daren didn't look as I sunk into a plush chair. The piano, a glorious black Cadillac of an instrument, stood between a potted palm and a bronze horse rearing back, waist high. The whole arrangement was framed on a Persian rug of gold, blue, and crimson; designs of crosses, lattices, stars. I watched Daren's bare feet knead the rug. She leaned toward the piano, her mouth shaping hard curves.

It made a picture. She sang in earnest, her pink nails clicking on the polished keys, eyes so focused they appeared slightly crossed. The quaver in her voice opened and I thought of the girl in the picture in her bedroom, and her life since then: a Sixties wedding, a Seventies divorce, a career for the great beyond. Her boyfriends: heavy pinstriped capitalists, over-ripe with cologne, ensconced in their luxury automobiles. Married men, philosophical about their wives. And more recently younger guys, younger than me, marathon runners, computer whizzes, impressed with their luck and wondering how they did it.

Her hands hit the keys harder and harder. Her hair — which was long and black in the high school photograph — clouded her brow in a pale shag. Points of moisture glittered around her eyes.

I remembered the afternoon she and Melba looked at my drawings. I hadn't known Melba long; I was meeting

Daren for the first time. I watched their hands on the sketch pad between them. Their eyes moved from page to page and they laughed, they laughed till the tears came. I realized I was falling for their laughter. Right then and there, as they touched my pictures, I knew everything was about to change.

The singing stopped. The piano fell silent.

She grasped the edge of the bench with both hands and stretched at the tension in her neck and spine.

"Impressive," I said.

She shook her hair from her eyes. "That was nothing," she said. "Arpeggio junk. Real music wouldn't sound half so good."

"I liked it," I said.

We looked at each other. The phones went off again, a clatter of fuzzy bells left and right.

"That's for me," she said, kicking back the bench. In heavy strides, ankles flashing beneath her robe, she disappeared into the hall. I heard a grim and forceful hello, followed by silence, then her lowered voice. I sat in the deep chair regarding the slender crescents her feet had left in the carpet.

In the hall, Daren said, "What are you telling me? Just tell me. Say it." Her voice went down again in a rush of breathless syllables, as if she'd reverted to a different language to make herself understood.

On the way to Melba's room I ducked into her father's office. I turned on the desk lamp and glanced at the stacks of papers, the cheap pens and smudged ashtrays. The swivel chair, pushed away from the clutter and facing the door, suggested he'd left on the run. I found the liquor cabinet above the standing file. Dozens of little airline bottles filled the top shelf. I jammed my pockets with four or five Wild Turkey miniatures and headed for the bedrooms, turning into Daren's open doorway — noticing the light under Mrs. M's at the end of the hall — then into Melba's room through the adjoining bath.

Melba hadn't actually lived here for years. The walls were bright with fish-shaped mirrors and framed watercolors of Paris street scenes. Over the bookcase hung a pen-and-ink portrait of a grinning Saracen or gypsy. The longer I looked at it the greater was my impression that Melba had known this man. He'd drawn himself and given it to her. I felt certain the grinner was real, and that he had her phone number.

I sat on the queen-sized bed and drained off a whiskey. I threw my clothes over a chair of polished mahogany and paced in my shorts, peering at Melba's books and knick-knacks from adolescence and childhood. I leaned into the long closet and brushed my arm over hanging rows of cotton jumpers and wool skirts, things she'd never wear again. A smell like cedar and perfume filled my head.

I stood and listened. I went to the bureau and laid my hand on the top drawer. Slowly I pulled and slowly the drawer opened, exposing soft pinks and blues, pastel sweaters and socks. In a corner, two maroon books with gilt pages and the word JOURNAL stamped on their spines. I hefted them in my hand. I tried to feel what they were about through their covers, and then I returned them to their corner. But I didn't shut the drawer. I stared at the books, the way the folded clothing seemed to buoy them toward the light. I took up one of the journals and stepped over to the floor lamp and opened it. It dated from Melba's university days, almost ten years ago.

The door rattled softly, someone tapping.

"Bruce, are you awake?"

I shoved the book under a pillow and cracked the door, squinting out.

Mrs. M smiled and nodded in the darkened hallway.

"Just about to call it a night," I said.

"Yes, I just wanted to say," she said, and she slipped into the room, blinking at the lamp, the mirror, me in my shorts. I cleared the chair for her.

"Do you mind?" she said, settling against its carved back. She was dressed for bed, but her face was rouged, her hair perfect. "About what I said earlier," she said. "Don't misunderstand. Don't take the wrong meaning."

"In what sense?" I said, standing before her.

She folded her hands on the lap of her nightdress, a gesture that Melba had inherited. Or perhaps Mrs. M had stolen it from her daughter.

"I don't want you to think I'm a worry wart, and I don't mean to put you on the spot, but I know Melba's happiness is important to you. Whatever is between you, I know you want good things for her."

"I do," I said.

"Yes, and her father is more hindrance than help. Let's face it, she gets support from other sources."

I shifted from foot to foot. "She has lots of friends," I said.

"Oh, I know. She certainly does. But she's almost thirty, Bruce. She needs a career. Something solid."

I nodded grimly. "Was Daren at that age?" I asked. "Solid, I mean."

Mrs. Marcroft frowned. She frowned so rarely it was surprised to see how it altered her presence.

She said, "Daren was married then. But you're right. She's had a time of it, too. Chiropractors, acupuncture, analysts galore. I guess this is the age we live in."

"I guess it is," I said. "But what about Melba?"

Mrs. M's eyes met mine. Her face was bright with concentration.

"Never mind," she said. She stood. "This isn't the time. I just didn't want you to misunderstand."

Through the closing the door she said, "Sleep tight, Bruce."

Tight, I thought.

I stood watching the door, then I brought out the journal. I paged randomly until an entry from a particular Sunday caught my eye.

Five of us in the car, three of them men I'd never met before. An afternoon to remember. One or two of these in a lifetime.

Directly before me on the bureau sat another photograph, about six by eight. Melba, head and shoulders. I happened to know it was taken in Rome three years ago. Except for the earrings you'd think, What a striking young man. Black hair combed back and razored over the ears like a baseball star from the Twenties. Something about the gemmy light in her eye, the determined jaw, made me think how blessed little I know about people. That they are, in fact, not egg-shaped or sad sack, like my drawings. Right now, the real Melba might be anywhere in the actual world. On the beach, or in the city; maybe just sitting in a diner and smiling at the talk she overhears. Just sitting there, she's perfect. Look at her. Look at that face, flushed and handsomely intent. Day going down behind her. You don't love a face like that. Love isn't the issue. But you want it close, like a talisman. Something to look on when you doubt.

I drank the last little bottle and lay on the bed. An anxious sleep caught up with me. When I woke a few hours later I felt haggard and strange. For an instant, lying there with my eyes open, I thought I wasn't alone.

I got up and felt my way to the bathroom. Daren's door was open, her light on. I saw the rumpled bed, the book on her pillow, her reading glasses on the nightstand. Her photograph smiled confidence and appeal. The black robe and her clothes were heaped on the chair. I stepped into the room. "Daren," I said. I lifted the robe and put it back. I sat on the bed and quickly stood again.

Turning away from the face in the picture, I made my way through the hall. I felt the closeness of the dark, the good thick carpet between my toes. I looked behind me at Mrs. M's door, kitty-corner to Melba's. I had the feeling that we were staring at each other through the door and the dark, and that as soon as I looked away she'd slip out. I kept going down the hall.

An open window in another part of the house admitted the faint ghost of a moan. I stopped in the parlor near the front door and listened. A small red light blinked in a panel on the wall. I tried to remember where to walk. I moved closer to the kitchen: the ghost sound seemed to come from the darkness outside, and I had the impression of a night draft through an open door down the corridors. But I turned away from the sound, and immediately a sort of relief passed through me. I forgot my sense of being followed by ghosts toward ghosts. I remembered Alfred. That was what it was like, not revelation or new light, but memory returning, and I knew the dog was mine.

As I stepped through the livingroom I passed the piano, black and sepulchral on four legs; the moan outside crested into an all-out wail, then broke into diminishing sobs that bubbled back into the darkness.

"Melba?" I said. "Daren?"

I could feel them, the women of this house, stirring in the night. I moved away from the piano and into the den.

I left the lights off and as I groped for my pencil I seemed to be holding my breath. The world would not look at another Rembrandt or admit a new Cezanne, but it had simpler rules for cartoons. Alfred, my lost beagle, called to me. I saw him, real dog, more than dog, trotting out of uncreated chaos. Footsteps in the other room, movement in the hallway. I kept my eye on Alfred. His ears flapped like old slippers; his tail came up like the tired salute of a wary, knowing father.

I squeezed the pencil in my palm. I wanted to show Daren what it was like. I wanted to send Alfred into the night after her. And like that, I had his first adventure. *Alfred In Love*, story of a Berkeley lady lawyer who fights for all the right causes, looks good, talks sharp, but owns a heart that won't stop breaking. It breaks and breaks, she doesn't know why. Until she meets Alfred. B-movie beginning that opens to ultimacy, self meeting self, the laughter of true liberation.

Outside, a woman's cry trembled and went to pieces. In the kitchen a voice answered, a chair toppled, and all at once the entire house went off, alarm upon alarm, shrill electricity slicing the dark.

"Watch this," I said. In a moment I'd reach for the light and begin.

But I stood there, making fists I couldn't see, while the house cried and cried as if it would come apart with pain.

LUSH
LIFE

When Trudy phoned that afternoon the winter light on the front window was fading: music rose from my basement and I heard cars outside coming home from work. Chet Baker and Gerry Mulligan played slow, laconic choruses of *Making Whoopee*. At first I thought she wanted to air out office politics or a deal gone sour, which could take an hour or more, and I put heat on under the coffee while she spoke. But then she mentioned Arthur.

"He's talking about quitting work," she said. She let it sink in and continued. "He says it's time for some changes. He says selling condos to young lawyers doesn't mean anything to him anymore."

"Well," I said.

"That's not the half of it, Burt. He's talking about taking up the piano again. He says he wants to get back into music."

She waited and I waited.

"I thought you could speak to him. You've been through the syndrome. I thought you might help him to make sense."

Arthur and Trudy have been living together for just over a year and I can honestly say I wish them well. I don't wish any travail their way. But I wasn't sure what she was asking me.

"He needs another man's point of view," she said. "Someone who's not in his field. Someone he trusts."

I could hear her noodling at the computer on the other end. The phone slipped and she swore distantly.

"This doesn't come at good time for me," she went on. "Things are tough in advertising right now. I don't know if you know what's happening out there, but this is not a good time. And I'm going nuts trying to quit the cigarettes."

I listened to her and the music from downstairs. The house was getting dark around me.

"Where are you now?"

"At work. Where else?"

"You sound tired."

"Listen, Burt. Think about what I'm saying. I thought you might tell Arthur what it would mean, giving up everything at this stage in his career. You could tell him how things are with you."

"Things are fine with me," I said.

It's true. These days my life is undeniably serene. My gettings up and lyings down are regular and devoid of yearning. The mornings are short and empty, the afternoons and evenings consumed in the benign art of typewriter repair in my basement shop. When I left Sun Life three years ago it was the first of a series of resignations, all of which brought me closer to the actual world and the rational music that exists without over-signifying, that comment without hope or despair.

"When did you get so hard to talk to? You used to be a wonderful talker, Burt. I don't know if you realize it, but once upon a time I loved to hear you talk."

"Not at the end, you didn't."

She snuffled, cleared her throat. "Anyhow," she said, "I don't expect you to take any position on this. I'd just like Arthur to have the opportunity to see you."

I wondered what Arthur would see that might change his mind, straighten him out. Obviously, Trudy feared this was déjà vu, that the revelation or malaise that had gotten hold of me had returned to claim Arthur. She didn't know if it was a genuine problem, a male thing, or just a copycat gesture.

"My situation was nothing like Arthur's. He's an entirely different person."

Although we both knew what it meant to be intimate with Trudy.

"But just talk to him, okay? Do it as a favor for me. All right? Can you do it for me?"

I heard someone come into the office behind her and say something. She put her hand over the receiver and replied, like underwater.

She came back and said, "Can you do it, Burt?"

"Sure."

She thanked me, gushing a little in the manner that got me down in our final days, and we arranged to meet at her favorite place in town, just after work next Friday.

In the evening I dined on rice and black beans and drank respectable red wine. I listened to Mozart and Ellington and for dessert ate cornbread I'd made the day before, with fresh coffee.

What could I tell Arthur? Life was not unhappy, alone and semi-employed. There are advantages not to be scorned. I tried to recall the last time I'd seen him. It was a party at someone's house where I met Arthur standing in the front yard, smoking a cigarette, drink in hand and his overcoat open. "It's a no smoking house," he said. He's a heavy guy, bear-like, but his hands are pale and slender. I noticed them as he smoked. We stood there several minutes, a wet snow falling sinuously through the darkness. I admired his camel hair coat and regretted the passing of indoor smoking, though it's a habit I've never had. He swayed slightly and stared at me, the snow gathering on his shoulders. A new gray beard made his face long and haggard, though he's just mid-fortyish, a few years older than me. "Trudy's inside talking to some kid from her office," he said. Then he asked me some questions about my marriage, where my ex-wife was, if we were still close. I told him I hadn't heard her voice in years; moreover, I didn't know for sure where she was living. He shook his head, as if this were hard news. He said, "Trudy and I used to talk about getting married. But I don't know what it means anymore. Marriage. What the hell does that mean, anyhow?"

Something like that. He asked his questions and then I went inside. I didn't get a chance to talk with him again that night.

That was weeks ago, right after Christmas.

I refilled my cup and took it downstairs and put on a new tape, Coleman Hawkins. Settling into the grease-stained La-Z-Boy, I regarded the typewriters, a dozen of them lining the shelves or in various stages of reconstruction on the benches. Olympia electrics from the late 60s, wonderfully substantial, like outboard engines waiting to roar. Underwood portables from the 50s, compact and heavy, darkly gleaming with good steel. Their common-sense parts under the fluorescents gave me a cool, solid feeling that matched the music. Never knew how much I loved music until I took up typewriter repair. It slowed things down, made me listen. No wonder Arthur wanted to sit at the piano again. Whatever his talent, it takes a spacial calm to hear it, to hear the notes arranged in time. You can't make it happen by chasing after it with your will.

Sure, sometimes I miss the sushi lunches, the artificial urgency and sublimated sexuality of the work place. Sometimes I miss the heady scent of lady execs in designer eyewear and imported heels, or the ironical fatigue of the younger guys, so cleanly shaven one skin seems to be missing. Most of all, I miss the mornings in the recently awakened world, the first stirrings of commerce in the downtown streets in summer. But I never regret leaving them behind. These days my blood pressure is like my income: steady and low. I work in the actual, receiving cash or personal cheque for each completed job. Fixing typewriters requires a basic knowledge, few tools, and patient hands. No computers or fossil fuel. No devotion to the company ideal or a larger vision of the global economy. However neglected, the typewriter is a pure machine.

Therefore, it will never be obsolete.

I drank my coffee and tried to keep the feeling of the music that swirled around my benches and chair. Trudy's voice interfered. It seemed to speed the music up and make the typewriters appear irrelevant and crude. The most casual contact with her has this effect on me, and I have to tell myself that she doesn't mean it. It's just her way. My reaction is strictly chemical.

Trudy, the woman I loved after my wife, has become my metabolic opposite. During our two good years immediately prior to my resignation, I often joked that she was impossible to photograph, that although her body might appear stationary her spirit was already en route to the next engagement, the next client or co-worker across town, and her image would turn out blurred. It was a joke based on a partial truth, an impression. But toward the end it seemed like a prophecy, or an epitaph, and I stopped and watched her spin away. Since then she's climbed the advertising ladder and she's busier than ever, moving faster, filling her calendars with names and events that serve as a graph for her earthly happiness.

For this reason, our encounters are few. Also, they are limited on principle.

Her kinetic orbit is powerful and it's difficult to meet casually without being sucked in and pulled along; it's nearly impossible to be in her company without being rattled by her most current concern, a concern which she may jettison before dinner, leaving you to brood on her behalf into the evening.

"Oh hell," I said, and I stood and turned off the lights, killed the music, and took my coffee upstairs. I emptied the cup in the sink and picked up the phone. Her number rang three times and then her recorded voice came on surprisingly subdued, almost sad, and I hung up. I went to the front window and looked out. The snow had stopped and a nearly full moon shone bluely on the unplowed streets and yards. They looked like smooth, blown dunes in a midnight Sahara.

I breathed out and closed the curtains.

Poor Trudy. It was wrong to judge her. She didn't live her life so much as pilot it frantically through the chutes. She was inside it, like a rocket or bobsled, fighting the controls. Her meaning was obtained through motion, not substance. Without the motion, the speed and crazy energy, she'd cave in on herself and perish.

Soon after midnight I left my bed and went to the kitchen for a glass of milk. Trudy and I never lived together; in fact, we never spent more than five or six nights together in our two years. Half a dozen, tops. Several afternoons a week we'd meet at her place, when she was working at the computer in her upstairs study. That's where she liked it, on the couch in her study. Often, she'd get right up and return to the console. The sight of her broad shoulders hunched at the computer filled me with a falling and inexpressible melancholy, like those public TV shows about contented Pygmies on the verge of being overwhelmed by civilization, or the ones about certain small whales swimming lonesomely on the outskirts of extinction. As the keys clicked away I'd find my pants and wander downstairs to start coffee.

I've often thought there's no such thing as sexual memory, but that picture of Trudy at the computer is all I can recall of those afternoons. I can't bring back the feel of her bare, athletic shoulders against mine or the hungry fit of her mouth. Whatever we had that impressed me as real and worthy of care and compromise is wholly gone. I can say it, I can vow it was there, but I can't feel it now.

"Long gone," I said, raising the tumbler of milk.

I finished it, rinsed the glass, and went back to bed.

On Friday I drove into town in the early evening and found a parking space near the building where Trudy works. There were lights on up there, though I didn't let myself look more than once. I spent half an hour walking, looking at window displays, experiencing the Friday night ebb and flow of shoppers, tired secretaries going home, couples on their way to dinner or shows. I told myself I had people to meet and places to go and let myself enjoy the relative mildness of the winter night. I tried to think about Arthur, what I'd tell him. Obviously, he shouldn't quit his job. Not belonging to city life has definite drawbacks. It's like a long freefall to be endured unblinkingly, a sensation of oblivion rushing up while your friends and accountants fly away, an oblivion that might arrive suddenly if you flinch. On the other hand, a bracing stroll in town is not the same as working there morning to night, and any soul might be forgiven for declaring, "Enough."

I checked the big clock on the bank and hurried toward the restaurant-bar where Trudy and Arthur would be.

I hung my coat in the lobby and looked inside. The size and hum of the crowd surprised me. The sound it made was big and worldly without being truly loud. I waded into it and kept my eyes open. Dodging waiters and manuevering around tables, I went to the end of the room and came back to the bar. No sign of Trudy or Arthur. As soon as I ordered a beer someone tapped my shoulders.

A woman I didn't know said, "Are you Burt? Are you looking for Trudy? She told me to tell you she'd be along in a few minutes, she got stuck at work, but if you want we can wait for her at my table . . ."

She was slim and authoritative, with streaked grey hair that matched her silver-grey suit. The suit was criss-crossed with shiny black buttons like bandoliers.

"How'd you know me?"

She smiled. "Trudy described you to a T."

I emptied the bottle into my glass and followed her to a table in the middle of the room. She moved through the sound of it in a way that reminded me of films from the mid-60s where continental women entered stylish restaurants to bossa nova soundtracks. Perfect secular beauties riding the zenith of their appeal in time.

"What happened to Trudy? Where's Arthur?"

She sipped her Scotch and raised her chin. "Ah, you know. Work. A bunch of calls from Trudy to Art charting their progress across town. He phoned just before I left her office."

Then she introduced herself, Marilouise Clow or Cloud, and explained that she and Trudy had done business together. She edited an architectural magazine that Trudy had placed advertising in, and now they swam together most Friday afternoons.

"Trudy's a strong swimmer," I said.

"Is she ever. I just do a few laps. She goes end to end without stopping and blows everybody else out of the water."

Now that she mentioned it, I noticed that her short, permed hair was still damp, and I knew that if she leaned closer I'd smell a taint of chlorine on warm, perfumed skin.

We sat and talked about Trudy and Arthur and the latest outfit in town to fold.

She asked me: "Is there any future in typewriters?"

I hadn't mentioned the repair business and the thought of Trudy telling her made me wince inwardly.

"Well," I said, "they have an honorable past. And if they have a future it's one I can live with. Nobody's going to blame the typewriter for juvenile delinquency or higher taxes."

I was trying to tell her that there was no danger of losing ourselves in typewriters, but the more I explained the more the topic appealed to me, and I heard myself taking faster and sharper, with a spin I'd forgotten I could throw.

"For my money," I said, "the best things our civilization invented, the things that will last, are the typewriter, the bicycle, and the saxophone."

Marilouise smiled and gave her hair a girlish toss. "The saxophone," she said. "Who invented that?"

I emptied my glass and said, "Sax."

She reached across the table and touched my hand. "I have to make one quick call. Why don't you have another drink."

I watched her rise and sail across the crowded room. And immediately a sadness struck like a tone, a quavering disenchantment that began in her image and spread through the restaurant and bar like a one-noted hopelessness that numbed my response, so I felt as though I were little more than an extension of the tables and chairs.

The waiter bowed to ask if I wanted another beer.

"Just the bill for the one I had."

When Marilouise returned I was standing, putting my wallet in my pocket.

"Oh," she said, with mild surprise and maybe disappointment.

"Sorry," I said. "I just realized the time." I reached and shook her hand. It was smooth and firm.

"If Trudy shows, tell her I couldn't wait."

She smiled neutrally and nodded. She stood there and watched while I walked out of the room, the human noise of it fading behind me.

Later that evening Trudy phoned to apologize. "As it turned out," she said, "Arthur couldn't make it. But tomorrow night he's playing the lounge at the Holiday Inn. It's his debut, Burt. He and his bass player will be there from nine until midnight. Could you come then? I think the sooner you speak with him, the better."

I tried to remember the last time I'd been in town on Saturday night. Over a year, probably. I agreed to meet them and got off the phone before she could tell me how much it meant to her or call me a good sport.

After supper I watched a documentary about shrimp and went to bed early. I slept a couple of hours and opened my eyes, wide awake. Without turning on the lights I checked each room and looked out the window through a freezing rain that hit the glass like pellets and crystallized there, blearing the view of the street and the neighbors' darkened houses.

It doesn't happen often, but on nights like this I'll let myself imagine being perfectly met in a lover, in a woman who wants to live free of hysteria and false meaning. Her vocation is practical and heartfelt. There's no imagining her without this vocation. Perhaps she has a job that requires steadiness and precision. Maybe she works with photographs and magnifying lenses, cleaning up images, taking out unwanted shadows and objects, even faces; replacing them with calm and light. She makes sanity out of clutter, as though she were removing hurts and seasons of hurt, not idealizing but restoring things to what they should have been, might have been, with a little luck and restraint. This woman does not live by business wits alone and when she speaks her voice is open and slow. Some nights I can hear it plainly while the rain hits the windows, and it's not hard to believe that she exists. But to keep the voice I must concentrate on her work. There's no sense of her without first establishing the exact nature of her employment. Although her voice is warm, imagining her work is what steers me into sleep.

The next night I drove down to the Holiday Inn on the waterfront and parked in the lot. A cold wind laced with thin snow came off the ice and water. At the automatic doors I seemed to be carried through on the rushing warmth of a vacuum, sucked into the carpeted pastel lobby of modulated lamplight and out-of-towners waiting at the desk. I followed signs in the corridor toward the lounge and spotted Trudy at a table near the gas fireplace. Closer to the bar, Arthur stood behind an electric keyboard, tuning with the bass player. Arthur wore a sober expression and a fuzzy brimmed hat I'd never seen before. When I came in Trudy was lighting a cigarette; she waved the spent match and expelled a cloud of smoke through a guilty grin.

"You caught me," she said. "Things have been so crazy, I couldn't quit. I guess another week or two of cigarettes won't kill me."

The waitress materialized immediately and I asked for a beer.

"Wait. Have a martini, Burt. It's on me. You used to love a good cocktail. I'm paying tonight.'

I thanked her and said, "I haven't had a martini since when."

"With me, I bet. You haven't had time for me for months, Burt. Last summer, I think."

She focused on me through the blue smoke and I saw that her hair was shorter, blonder, and it made something golden and classical of her face. Probably she'd been going to the tanning spa.

"It's not like that," I said. "You're the one on the tight schedule. I just don't come into town that often anymore."

She frowned briefly. She said, "I've been telling every-one that you're the man for typewriter repair in this town."

In fact, her recommendations had landed me some machines. I mentioned this and asked after her own work.

She shoved her chair back and groaned musically. She wore French jeans and suede boots and her burgundy cloth jacket had golden threads running through it.

"Funny thing about advertising," she said. Sometimes it needs a light touch. Just a touch. Other times you have to lean and punch. Lately, it's been a punch-out."

My martini came around and I raised it to her.

"I hope you're winning," I said.

"I win my share." Then she straightened and looked past me. I turned: Arthur was inclined toward the key-board, listening absorbedly.

"Anyhow," Trudy said, "Marilouise enjoyed meeting you. You know, we swim here. Just down the hall, every Friday afternoon. Another woman from the office comes, too. You should join us." She laughed. "But maybe it wouldn't be your cup of tea."

I sipped my drink. I knew she was seeing me in a pool full of motivated women, strong swimmers, going around and around.

Trudy blanked her cigarette and said, "Damn these things, anyhow. Damn me for being weak willed."

"You're anything but. Will is your specialty."

She looked around the room. She said, "I hope Arthur will open up with you a little, Burt. I'm running out of ideas. Tell him he sounded good, but remind him how tough it's getting. Just tell him how it is with you."

"I keep telling you. It's not bad with me."

She sniffed and looked away. "I bet the acoustics are lousy in here."

The lights dimmed and Arthur began to play. The bass player pitched in furiously. Continuous fusion stuff. Original material, Trudy said. Arthur stood at the keyboard with his chin nearly resting on his chest, his hat shading his eyes. Sometimes they seemed to be closed. Sometimes he spoke a short, encouraging word to the bass player. The latter, balding and goateed and sporting a jade earring, worked the frets with the maximum expenditure of energy. Now and then he leaned to make an adjustment on the small, black amp between them.

Trudy watched and listened silently, shoved back in her chair, lifting an arm to smoke or drink or signal another round. I traded my empty for a fresh martini and thanked her. She paid with a wad of bills and waved off the change.

Arthur and his partner were working up some steam. Now and again drinkers and talkers situated around the room glanced at them with annoyance or curiosity. Arthur jammed back the sleeves of his black satin jacket and rocked on his heels. An unhealthy-looking sweat stood on his brow. The bass player hopped from foot to foot. The harder Arthur worked, the farther back he leaned on his heels, his middle thrust forward against the keyboard.

I drank the second martini too fast and reached for Trudy's glass of water. She watched the duo with a face of somnolent intensity and smoked without stopping, as if she were eating it, gulping it down.

The set ended on a seemingly arbitrary note. A sprinkling of applause mixed with the crackle of the fire behind us.

"That wasn't so bad," Trudy said.

Arthur slowly made his way to our table. He sat and folded his hands.

Trudy said, "Arthur, that was good!"

He looked at her, then at me. There was a boyish softness around his eyes that didn't match the salt-and-pepper beard.

"It was good," I said.

"Next set we'll try something different," he said. The waitress inquired if he needed anything and he shook his head. He asked me how it was going and remarked that his partner had an old Smith Corona that needed work.

"Give him my number. Spread the word."

He smiled faintly. "I will."

"Arthur," Trudy said, and she waited for him to look at her. "You and Burt should get into the fitness center here. Really. You get to use the pool and the bikes and the universal. We did their Christmas campaign. They'd probably give you a rate if you mentioned me."

Arthur watched her talk as if she were an emissary from another race or time, an Etruscan come to the end of our epoch to fetch cigarettes.

I said, "I've found that a solid reputation is the best advertisement. Word-of-mouth is still where it's at in typewriter repair."

Trudy blinked at me as if she wasn't quite sure I had spoken.

Arthur turned to locate his partner and said, "Good to see you, Burt. Maybe you'll be around later."

He crossed the room and began helping the bass

player set up an extra microphone near the keyboard.

"See?" Trudy said. "See what I mean?" She sat back and lit a cigarette. "He can't concentrate. He won't sit still."

"He looked pretty calm to me."

"He refuses to focus. He drifts. Something's been eating him for weeks."

As the music started Trudy seemed resigned to wait it out and enjoy her drink. Arthur was right. This set was different. They were playing torch songs and campy ballads I'd nearly forgotten. On the third number Arthur leaned toward the microphone.

"Oh God, he's going to sing," Trudy said.

Arthur touched the mike and started in: his voice was low and moist, loaded with unction. He cocked his head slightly, so he seemed to be peering at the audience from the corner of his eye under his hat.

"Oh God," Trudy said.

He sang *The Shadow of Your Smile* while the bass player swayed and people came and went and muttered and set their glasses on the tables. Someone turned the lights a little lower. The bass took a solo while Arthur hummed into the microphone. Then he played the chorus in grandiose chords for the finish, singing, "Now when I remember spring, and all the joys that love can bring, I will be remembering . . ."

Trudy raised her glass and beckoned to the waitress.

"That wasn't bad," I said.

They started the next number with hardly a break. Now there were no more than nine or ten of us in the darkened room, and I felt that the others — older couples and solitary business travelers nursing beers — were attending to the music as if unable to break the sweet-sad inertia long enough to escape to their rooms.

The song he was singing was familiar: I knew the tune and the words, but I couldn't name it. The title was there, just off to the side, under the table or in the shadows behind the keyboard, but I couldn't say it. It was about drinking and disenchantment with romance and tripping to Paris to relieve the humdrum. The words rhymed nicely and predictably, but the way he sang them added up to something new in Arthur and the song. In meaning and sentiment they were suddenly felt and unexpectedly believable. Perfectly met.

Trudy moaned softly. In the dimmed light her golden aspect had gone sallow, the shape of her face become the literal figurement of her pain.

What's left of love in this world? I can barely remember my wife, and though I try to imagine that other woman who may come along, immanent and calm and graceful of hand, I can't see her face. I can't feature her in my mind. The face I recognize, the face that is beside me in the dark for a short time, is Trudy's.

She rocked slowly and held herself, yearning toward Arthur or the long tremulous note of his song.

IN CHRIST THERE IS NO EAST OR WEST

In California they come at you on their bicycles, the white-shirted boys with their ties flying over their shoulders: Mormons or Jehovah's Witnesses or Young Republicans for Christ. I'm walking down a narrow suburban sidewalk, between the palm trees and the rock gardens, when they come at me from the street. Their eyes are beads of black light set in pink masks, American cupid faces, round and blemishless and perfectly naked.

"Hello there!" one shouts, like a war cry, and they shoot around me, one on either side in a slap of sharp air and light.

For a moment I stand and watch them pedal away. I take a step, and another, and I'm walking again, toward home on the dark side of town. These young missionaries have ridden their bikes from the bad heart of my neighborhood where they spend their days. They see it unravelling from month to month. They thrill in the absolute proof of God's plan, history's inevitable slide. They do not believe in gentrification or government aid. Instead, these boys laugh at the citizens whose indifference has handed them power. They are the stumbling block that was not seen. Tonight, in a clean motel, they will sleep on the lulling hum of a tremendous power, on the certainty of their stock in a great destructive machine and their status in what comes next.

Home, I smoke a cigarette on the back porch which I share with the college girl next door. Our kitchen doors are side by side. We enjoy living on the second floor, above the dust and rowdiness of the street. Liz regards me as a kindly but eccentric uncle or older brother. Her comings and goings are refreshing to me. She is busy and intelligent, a dark blonde who wears men's T-shirts and unfashionably tattered jeans. She understands music. She reads Camus and Cyril Connolly, and loves the idea of culture's richest veins opening for her here, in the midst of these squalid facts. Our building, for instance, is a four unit stucco affair surrounded by half a dozen trees gone rank and jungly; between the road and the front entrance there is no lawn, only weeds, and old newspapers, and the dank carpet of dead things from the trees. The building faces a long, yellow complex of garden apartments inhabited by illegal aliens and bikers. The street is lined with abandoned cars up on blocks and overflowing dumpsters. On weekends Liz rushes up and down the back stairs with cameras around her neck and skinny, half-frightened university boys in tow. She says she came here to escape the high rents, but I wonder: she drives a brand new Saab, white as a sugar cube, and once a month she flies to Los Angeles.

What happens on the street interests her. She isn't afraid.

And despite all this unsavoriness, our back porch is not a bad place to be on an autumn evening. The moon catches between ragged eucalyptus branches; the cold menthol air carries the muffled roar of coastal traffic and the classical music on Liz's stereo. I'm grateful for her healthy presence after the hysterical couple that lived there last year. The woman moved out after the police took her husband away in handcuffs. That was on Christmas Day. Jessica was with me then; we were eating turkey when the cruisers pulled up outside. We saw everything from the front window, with wineglasses in our hands.

I snub out my cigarette on the plank railing and knock on Liz's door. The music, Mahler or Brahms, is loud and she doesn't hear me. For a minute I wait, then go inside my place, turning off lights and undressing as I move toward the bathroom. There I draw a hot bath and lower myself into the tub. For an hour I soak in the dark. I light another cigarette and watch the vague smoke rise with the steam. My mind is stuck in neutral and my body is falling away.

I hear myself snoring lightly through clenched lips. The cigarette is drooping and I start awake when hot ashes hiss in the water around my neck. In the steamy dark I get out and towel off. I pull on a sweatshirt and boxer shorts and walk from room to room turning on lights. I sit at the portable typewriter and start a letter to my father. He lives in another part of the country. Mostly, this is helpful, but sometimes I'd like to see him, if only to remind myself of who I am.

As I type I notice that my fingernails need clipping; they're growing like crazy these days. Toenails, too. My body is a cosmos out of control, an ecosystem in anarchy; its chaos intersects and coincides with the confusion of our planet. It puts me in mind of the question I asked in seminary school: Is apocalypse personal or historical? The professor, a man renowned for his randy jokes and unoriginal thinking, replied, "Both, but that doesn't stop the world from starting over again."

I write:

Dear Dad:

Thanks for the cognac and playing cards. How did you know? I read the Emerson piece you suggested, the one about the Transparent Eyeball. Damn good. Highly excellent. I couldn't find the Johnny Hodges record but I came across an Art Pepper reissue that is truly fine. Did you see the Rangers beat the Black Hawks in Chicago? That goalie is a miracle, smooth as oil. I saw the last period at the bar. Still no work, but I'm playing better than ever. Don't forget what we talked about your checks and call me collect next month.

Your son,
Vincent

After I seal the envelope I realize that I'm wearing my father's underwear, hand-me-down shorts with little red scimitars and swastikas across the waistband. This cheers me and I go to the kitchen for the cognac that came UPS two days ago. Already the bottle is half empty, but I fill the bottom of a tumbler and toast my father who has all his marbles and gets thrown out of nursing homes for practising the clarinet and riling his cronies with talk about Gray Power and sex after seventy. He is a liberal of the old school and will not allow his heart to be broken by donzels and fools. He did not discourage my theological ambition, but clearly my father was pleased when I went back to the trombone.

"There's still a place in this country for a sharp bop trombonist," he said.

I don't believe this, but still, I play.

I toss off the cognac and step outside again. All's still next door. I knock briskly and this time she opens, smiling and blinking as if she's never seen me in my boxers before.

"There you are," says Liz. "How was the audition?"

"Fine, but these people want someone to fill in the spaces. They want sandwich sound. Anybody can do it. They know I'd be tempted to show off if I got the job."

She opens the fridge and hands me a bottle of beer.

I say, "Thanks. Could I borrow those piano concertos?"

"Concerti," she says. "Sure, but the recording isn't great."

We wander into her living room. Its primary furnishings are a spineless couch and a wicker armchair. A string of tiny blinking lights hangs from the ceiling, sparkling across posters of foreign cities and Diane Arbus photographs.

"Your posters are better than mine," I say.

"Here it is," she says, handing me the album. "Take these, too." And she hands me two more. I look at the jackets: *Einstein On the Beach* and a spanking new press of Beethoven's sonatas with Emanuel Ax and Yo Yo Ma. Liz's taste and knowledge are astonishing. Her blood is rich with culture. It seems to promote her complexion and the sunny burnish of her hair. She is twenty-one and I am thirty-four. We are on opposite ends of the supply and demand. She takes photographs and buys records. I play trombone all day. She says she can hear it through the walls.

She flashes a magazine in front of me and says, "I've been reading this article on the eugenics cult of the first half of this century. Amazing."

"I don't even want to know," I say. "That stuff frightens me plenty."

She laughs. She says, "But it's interesting. There's so much talk about race these days."

"Let's talk about something else."

We step back into the kitchen. I study the dinner plates in her sink. I sniff the air.

"There's a smell like dogs coming up through my

pipes," I say. "It's the spaniel downstairs. I bet it died and the old lady hasn't noticed."

Liz shrugs.

"Why don't you stop over later on?" she says.

As she closes the door she smiles as though she'll laugh the moment it clicks shut. I stand on the porch in the dark, the chill coming through my shorts. I hear Liz inside; she moves a chair and almost immediately her telephone rings. It chirps like a bird and she answers it cheerily. Below me, in the driveway, the moon floats like icebergs in the black puddles. Liz's voice moves around her apartment. She speaks rapidly and each silence is followed by bright laughter.

In my own kitchen, I put the beer in the refrigerator with the others. The middle level is almost full of frosted, amber bottles.

That night, I dream of Jessica, who shared this bed only five months ago; I dream we're in an Italian restaurant and there's a bad scene between us. I shout and throw my water glass against the wall. Two men, one tall and the other short, appear behind me. Both are balding and wear red flannel shirts with diamond studs in the cuffs and collars. They work for Mr. Polara, Jessica's boy friend. They say he wants to see me, outside. I shake my head but they lift me by the elbows and usher me around the corner. I try to scream. I know Polara will break my arms.

I wake with the blankets around my head. I catch my breath and feel my way to the living room to sleep on the couch. Back east, right now, Jessica will be starting her day, leaving the house of a man I've never seen, whose name is not Polara. A man who knows, perhaps, of my self-pity and absurd rages. Or maybe she tells him nothing. That's what I'm hoping as I slip back into sleep.

A fervent knocking rouses me from the couch. The drawn curtains are full of sunlight. I groan hell and damnation and, cinching my robe tight, I fumble toward the front door.

The man on the landing is not unnerved by my appearance. Squinting in the sun I see that he's tall and black; he wears black clothes and shoes that shine like black paint. His hand proffers some kind of pamphlet. I can't read the print but each black finger is studded with a silver ring.

"No," I say and I start to close the door.

His hand moves fast, fingertips pressed firmly to the door, just enough to keep it ajar. He looks hard into my eyes — not asking, staring for time — but he doesn't speak a word.

"Sorry," I say, and I shut the door.

For a moment I hold my eye to the peephole. He's still out there with that same look of righteous incredulity, his hand still stretched toward me, as if he's looking right back at me through the peephole.

Back on the couch I stretch out and sigh. Five minutes and I'm almost asleep, when he knocks again, louder this time.

"Honestly," I say and I rush the door, throwing it open to the clean-cut young man, handsome and straight and definitely white, who flashes me a smile as though a haggard face in a bathrobe is precisely what he's been waiting to see. He extends his hand.

"Mr. Pomeroy," he says. "It's a swell morning."

"Who are you?"

"I'm here to talk to you," he says.

He stands in the brightness of the new day, smiling. I lean out the door and look from side to side.

"Where's your friend?"

"I work alone," he says. "I stopped by yesterday, but you were out."

"Yesterday?"

He nods and once again offers his hand. He wears a white shirt with half sleeves and a tasteful blue tie. A good smell, like soap and rubbing alcohol, comes off him and suddenly it hits me that he's a dead ringer for Liz. A taller male Liz with black hair. But the face is hers, line for line.

"It's for a good cause, Mr. Pomeroy. I'm here to talk to you about your future, and the future of this town."

I don't want to, but I shake his hand. He has light in his eye and when he smiles all his teeth show. They're good teeth, white as pearls and regular as bathroom tile.

"You can trust me," he says, and then, laughing: "By the way, I like your robe. What color do you call that?"

I look down at my robe. "Yellow," I say. "I call it yellow."

"Or goldenrod. That's a good name for a color."

His smile isn't the least indulgent. He reaches out and touches my sleeve. There's some dried ketchup near his finger and suddenly I'm embarrassed in front of this proper young man.

"All right," I say. "Come on in. But make it brief. This goes against my better judgment."

He shows me his teeth, his innocence and zeal, and he darts through the doorway with surprising quickness. Before I can fix the latch he's getting comfortable on the couch, dropping my blankets in a heap on the floor.

"Thanks, Mr. Pomeroy," he says. "You have a real nice place here. I like the arrangement."

I say, "Talk. You've got five minutes. I have a mid-morning appointment."

"What about coffee?" he says. "Have you had coffee yet?"

I frown at him and tug my robe at the shoulder.

"You make coffee and I'll talk," he says. He grins with an earnest eye.

"Okay, let's hear it," I say, and I move into the kitchen and put the kettle on. He's quiet out there. I fix the filter in the cone and I step into the living room with pot in hand. His eyes are closed, his clean hands folded; his elbows are planted on his knees. He looks up and smiles.

"How's that coffee coming?"

"What did you say your name was?"

He shakes his head and folds his arms. "You don't trust me, do you? You really can't let go of your suspicions."

"I trust you," I say. "I trust everybody. Now please leave."

He's still shaking his head.

"I'm not getting through, am I?" he says. "Mr. Pomeroy, I'm here for a purpose, and you owe it to yourself and your neighbors to hear me out. There's a change coming, and you have to face it."

He's planted behind the coffee table, as if daring me to come after him.

"Listen," I say, "don't start with me. I spent a year in seminary. I've read the Bible the way some people read TV Guide." I can feel myself getting mad. "I see you guys working this side of town. Why don't you walk a few blocks and try that line on those rich people. Tell them about this big change."

While I speak he smiles at me, beatifically, tolerant.

"What difference east or west?" he says. "The work will go on where it will."

I point at the door.

"Out," I say. "Now. Please."

"Mr. Pomeroy, what's wrong? You've got trouble, am I right? A woman maybe? Where is she now? You can trust me."

The kettle starts to whistle. I press my palm against my forehead.

"I'm sorry," I say. "I have work to do. I need to be alone."

"Sure," he says. "Not to intrude. A quick cup of java and I'm gone. Relax now."

"All right," I say, and I shuffle out to fill the pot.

Sometimes I get confused. I forget that I have specific goals on earth. I forget that there are people out there who understand my frame of mind. But the way this boy says my name makes me want to renounce all the old ways, the old music, and begin again.

I return with two cups and set one down before him on the low table. He's sitting on the edge of the couch, arms crossed on his knees, leaning forward eagerly.

"Have any cream?" he says.

"No cream."

"Half'n'half?"

Our eyes meet for a moment.

"Black is fine," he says and he lifts the cup to his face and breathes in the aromatic steam. He sips from it. "Good," he says. "You make a wicked cup of coffee, Mr. Pomeroy. You're not drinking."

"I will," I say. "After you leave."

I settle in the armchair and watch him drink.

When his cup is half empty he looks around the room. He nods at the trombone case in the corner.

"You're a musician," he says.

"That's right."

He says, "May I?" And he springs across the room and crouches over the case, working the clasps with his hands.

I open my mouth, but I don't protest. Deftly he puts the trombone together and makes a breathy sound in the mouthpiece.

"It's a fine instrument," he says and he raises the bell toward the window and runs through a couple of scales. Without breaking stride he launches into song. He plays tunes I recognize: *Stardust* and *On A Clear Day*. He plays the Johnny Carson theme, and *A Taste of Honey*. He plays effortlessly; his hands know the positions as if this were as natural as eating with a fork and spoon.

He lowers the trombone and smiles at me, a little sheepishly. I sit there with my hands spread on the arm rests, the full cup of coffee on the floor between my feet. I feel shabby and not young. This boy can play.

"Don't stop," I say. "Let's hear more."

He smiles and hefts the instrument. He plays a sweet,

liquid tone; I don't know the titles but these are old hymns, melodies my father played at weddings and funerals. The room seems to fill with golden light and the boy plays as if he's been sent from God to take me home.

He finishes and looks at me over his shoulder, triumphantly.

"That's good," I say.

"Consider the future. My advice is make your peace with this world," he says. "Don't sleep on enmity."

And then, quickly, he disassembles the trombone, carefully placing each part in the case's red plush grooves. He snaps it shut and steps over to my chair. Before I can rise he leans over and pumps my hand.

"Thank you, Mr. Pomeroy. Thanks for the coffee and your time. Remember what I said. Don't sleep on it."

He smiles and withdraws his hand and almost instantly disappears behind the door, closing it softly after himself. I'm in the chair with my fingers locked on the rests and I'm listening hard, listening for the music he made in my living room's stale, morning air.

Later, I hear Liz climbing the back stairs. Her door slams. I pull on a clean shirt, lace my sneakers, check in the mirror. I step out and tap on her door. She calls from the other room and I open the door. In the living room I find her sprawled on the chair, her legs in blue pedal-pushers stretched towards me. Her face seems pensive, abstracted. With my eyes on her white ankle socks and red moccasins I say hello. I stare and she doesn't speak.

At last she says, "Well?"

I shrug. I say, "I like your shoes. How was your day?"

"Awful," she says. "I'm angry. You want to know what about? I'm angry at myself, for being lazy. I'm angry at how easy it is for other people to paint pictures and write books. I want to *make* something."

"So make," I say.

She grimaces and sniffs. "Easy for you to say. I heard you playing over there this morning. You were really making music over there. I heard you.

I look at the posters on the wall behind her.

"It takes practice," I say.

"But still, to rip through a dozen songs like that. You made it sound easy. I'd give anything to play like that. There's more than talent or practice involved. It takes a state of mind."

I shrug. She looks at me, brows contracting.

"Are you all right, Vincent? You don't look right. Are you ill?"

"I haven't been outside today. I need fresh air, that's all."

She sighs and runs her hand through her hair. Her nails are pink and shapely.

"To tell the truth," I say, "I've been thinking about Jessica back in upstate New York. I've been thinking how important it is to have one person who sees the world the same."

Liz looks away, frowning slightly.

"You asked too much of her," she says. "You expected too much."

"What do you mean? You never even met her."

"But I know you."

"I screwed up, sure. But I never lost faith."

Liz looks at me and shakes her head. She says, "Faith? Faith in what? The poor woman needed some stability. You play the trombone, for God's sake. It's not complicated."

"Wait a minute. A moment ago you were telling me how much you wanted to play. You wanted music in your life."

She stretches in the chair, arms splayed over the sides.

"That's got nothing to do with it," she says. "All this talk about faith isn't going to solve your problems. You've got to take care of yourself. You've got to live in the world."

I shake one of her Marlboros from the pack and roll it between my fingers. "Just the same, when the world comes apart you need one person to see it through with you."

Liz says, "But it's you that's coming apart, not the world. You know what I'd do if I were you? I'd get a loan and buy a car. That's Step One to living in the Twentieth Century."

She dangles a red moccasin from her toe. Her legs are celebrations, like Christmas in a wealthy house.

The next afternoon I'm walking home from another audition, taking my time along the quiet sidestreets with their well-tended homes. All last night the rain fell and the lawns are electrical green; the trees and gardens full of a dark potency. In front of a low sweeping house of crystal and stone an old Chinese man is cleaning out the pedestal birdbath. He wears a plaid flannel shirt and a porkpie hat. His face is white and faded. He works meticulously, with expressive white hands, as if he were concerned with the happiness of birds rather than the order of domestic land-scape. And I think of my father, that hot old man, playing Sidney Bechet on a phonograph that looks like a battered typewriter case. His room has a window that opens on an eastern city where it might be snowing, blue snow falling drowsily against gray brick walls.

The light jumps and tears; the missionary boys on their bikes fly over pavement as if they've been flung from the sky. In a moment of ideal geometry I'm caught between them and the gardener. He steps into a shadow and the boys swoop in, shoulder to shoulder, their bright faces growing larger, brighter.

My will dissolves and snaps back solid.

"Come on," I say, and I level the trombone case at my hip, holding it as though it were a lifeline, a rocket, an engine that will pull me through the clean, white space between their hearts.

SOLDIERS ON THE LAKE

Spence turned the open book on its face and listened to the laughter that drifted through the night from the cottage a hundred feet away. He turned off the lamp and parted the curtains. There were no lights on in there, but undoubtedly the women were still up, sharing a few minutes of intimate talk before ending their day. He felt a surge of dumb anger, then sighed it off. No point in contending with himself. If the situation didn't entail an implicit rejection he might enjoy sleeping out here in the shack. He liked the closeness and the roughness of the space, just big enough for a kitty-corner cot and bed, and a small writing desk beside the woodstove. Two windows and a door. The bed was beneath a shelf of old lanterns and rusted fishing reels. No carpet, no paint on the walls. It was perfect, only he had the lingering half-conscious impression that he should be in the cottage, in Christine's bed.

The given reason — which Christine proferred unequivocally and Spence pretended and tried to accept — was that sharing her bed would offend her fourteen year old daughter, Nathalie, who was still unwilling to believe her mother's relationship with him was anything but casual.

"I don't want to make my daughter watch me perform," Christine said. But Spence had no intention of making anyone watch, and he suspected she was using the girl to protect her own highly private psychic territory.

He turned the light back on. The book which he had brought from the used book store where he worked was some kind of odd science fiction prophecy from the early 1920s. Its functional conceit was a vision of eastern rural Ontario in the year 2000 as the home and secret stronghold of a powerful paramilitary organization known as the Phelanian Knights. The faded covers depicted a piney northern lake beneath a stern, medieval-looking flag. The frontispiece picture of the author showed a surprisingly handsome, youngish man in a neat suit. The resolution of the photograph enhanced the depth of his eyes and the gloss of his oiled, black hair. Dr. Eustace R. Merrill would be long dead and no longer deluded, Spence thought, but he felt an awkward stab of envy for the figure in the book. Spence had an idea that this man would be faring much better with the women in the cottage across the way than he had in the last day and a half.

He closed the book and folded his hands behind his head. The simple truth was that he was out of his element here in the woods, on the lake. He valued the quiet and the opportunity to get clear of the city in summer, but what he had to offer was somehow diminished by the landscape. It wasn't just the raw facts of nature, it was the history of the place, the private mythology of it that Christine carried in her head. She'd been coming here since she was a child, and it meant something to her that Spence would never be able to share or penetrate. His stock of stories and witticisms fell dead on these austere pine bluffs and pools. The very water — steaming in the mornings, muttering into silence at night — seemed to belong to Christine alone or present a mystery which only she could translate. It was this seeming mystery that stole the vitality from his speech, the meaning from his own store of memories.

Yesterday he had tried telling Vera, Christine's friend who was visiting from New Zealand, about something that had happened to him as a graduate student in Baltimore seven years ago, a night when his life, or at least his health, had been saved by a black transvestite outside a harborfront tavern, how she/he had produced a mean little gun from his/her handbag and how the gang had backed off, melted into the darkness. It was a story he had told Christine at one of their first meetings, a story that had charmed and intrigued her. But up here it was rendered void by the spirit of place, by the presence of the lake which held canyons of cloud and low-flying herons. As he and Vera sat on the dock, with Christine swimming around them, the world of his story refused to signify.

Vera smiled and went inside to make tea, while Christine backstroked into the distance.

He reached for the light and the cabin went black. The laughter had stopped and there was nothing to hear but tiny snaps and cracks and something like the elongated respirations of the earth itself, something that was there only if you didn't listen for it.

In morning he woke to the scuttling of chipmunks or squirrels on the cabin's roof. He rose groggily, pulled on his pants and made his way barefoot down the path toward the cottage. Already a sweet and resinous warmth was rising form the woods; the green weeds and dead branches and the trodden dirt path were crisscrossed by slashes of golden light. The rough vegetable garden had recently been watered and he heard drops plopping on broad leaves; small butterflies hovered between turgid green stalks.

He opened the screen door and called good morning to no response. From the screened porch adjoining the kitchen he saw Vera stretched on a towel down on the dock and Nathalie dangling her feet in the water, hunched over a book. Out in the bay, Christine swam toward them. She was training. She'd never competed before, but her boss had asked her to represent the company in the swimming leg of the city triathalon and she had resolutely accepted, as if the fact of a middle-aged woman's swim-racing that far might distinguish not only her office but her gender to boot.

Spence frowned and squinted against the morning light that came off the lake in brilliant splinters. He stepped into the kitchen and lifted the coffee pot on the stove. The pot was half-full and hot. He poured himself a cup and added evaporated milk. Moving to the porch, he watched Christine stroking toward the dock in a strong, straight line with no wake.

He let the door slam and started down the embankment with his coffee cup. The moment his foot touched the warm dry wood of the dock Christine rose up from the shining water and called out, "Good morning, Spencer." Vera, baking on her back, repeated the greeting.

Spence said, "Good morning. Hello. What's the book?"

Nathalie peered up at him as if she'd heard something far away, blinked, and returned to her reading.

"I don't know why I'm doing this." Christine breathlessly hoisted herself upon the dock. She shook her hair and flopped on her side, the water streaming off and darkening the weathered planks.

"Because a man dared you," Spence said.

"I think it's wonderful," Vera said, still on her back, her expression impenetrable behind her round, dark glasses. "You're just threatened, Spencer. You don't like the idea of Christine competing."

This seemed a peculiarly confrontational line from a woman he hardly knew. He shook his head and looked away.

"Not true," he said. "You think she's doing this for women everywhere. But really it's for her pride. She wants to be one of the guys."

"I think you're afraid somebody will notice her."

"What do you mean, notice her?"

"Hey," Christine said.

Vera slipped the glasses off and turned over. With one hand behind her she undid the strap and slid the suit down to her waist, exposing the thin shaft of her back, her spine in pronounced relief. Before she arrived Christine had explained to Spence that Vera had nearly died of cancer, more than one kind, several years ago. She'd lost a breast. Her husband had left her for dead and disappeared to Finland with a younger woman. After all that, Spence thought, she doesn't have to be pleasant.

"Anyhow," Christine said, laying her arm across her forehead as she settled back, "it's getting me into shape."

"There are easier ways," Spence said.

He waited for Vera to answer, but her face was averted. It struck him as noteworthy that a woman who had battled cancer would soak in the morning sun. He stepped around Nathalie and squatted at the dock's end, his back to the three women. He gazed across the water to the green edge of the far shore. The roofs of one or two distant cottages caught the sun. A few boats, tiny and buglike, were visible below them. The only other human reference in the vicinity was an occasional bell or distant hymn from the new Christian camp on the hidden south side, a community Christine loudly excoriated for polluting the lake's spiritual purity.

Spence filled his chest with clean air and watched the small fish that flashed in the green shallows. He regretted trading words with Vera first thing in the morning. That was the part that disturbed him, that he had risen to the bait this early in the day.

Suddenly he had that feeling of displacement, that

nearly visceral loss of balance that accompanied the dead-on apprehension of a simple fact. Christine would never let him in. He knew that. They had good sex on deserted afternoons in empty houses, they had lively conversations over wine in ferny bars and restaurants, but she would never admit him into her real life. Her myth of self was powerful and exclusive; it rose from a deep subterranean heart, like mist in the woods or wind off the lake.

"For God's sake, Nathalie."

Spence turned.

Christine was dabbing at Nathalie's face with a wet towel. Vera lifted her head and watched. Blood, thick blood, streamed from Nathalie's nose. Red drops fell on the page she continued to read.

"Just look this way a moment. Just for a moment," Christine said.

Spence heard a note of panic in her voice, a high and rare tone of disarray.

Vera said, "You might put the book down for a second, dear."

Nathalie was still reading and the blood kept coming, thick and bright in the morning sun. Finally her mother forced her to lie back, only then staunching the flow with the wet towel. But Nathalie kept reading, the towel pressed to her nose with one hand, the book held over her face with the other.

Preparing lunch was a relief, a neutral activity that put them all on the same wavelength. Spence and Vera were careful to joke with each other as he made salad and she put sandwiches on the table. Christine came out of the bedroom in sandals and a white linen robe, her composure restored. She hummed as she set the table, and as they ate she told stories about her early years on the lake. Nathalie interrupted to describe a dream she'd had last night, something about traveling with her mother to an island in outer space. The women listened attentively and asked questions. When Spence interrupted to tell about an altercation he'd had with a street person in his bookstore the other three looked at him as if he had broken some rule of cottage etiquette by referring to workaday life. Remembering how he'd bombed with the Baltimore story, he let this one drop.

"No, tell us," Vera said, refilling her wine glass.

Christine glanced at him with her implacable blue eyes.

"I honestly forgot what I was going to say," he said. "I lost my train of thought."

He told himself that Christine's distance was mostly her way of maintaining control, a tried-and-true method of protecting her role and place. He thought about this while they talked and ate. Ultimately, he decided, maintaining one's place was boring. If that's all she was about, he wouldn't be here. But her history was other. Over in New Zealand, where she'd spent her married thirties, she'd had a lover, a young Maori Ph.D. who did stress management workshops for fellow tribesmen. She described the relationship to Spence as exotic and impassioned, free from quotidian worries. But Nathalie hadn't a clue it had happened, and her father, Christine's husband from that time, was long gone.

After lunch Nathalie went into the bedroom to read

in private. Spence and the women moved to the porch with glasses of wine.

"We should swim across the lake," Vera said. "If you hadn't done it this morning, I'd say we should all swim the distance."

Christine shrugged. "I could do it again."

As if to get him off the hook, Christine asked Vera about common friends back in Wellington. Spence appreciated their effort to explain certain individuals and personalities to him. Each one had been a character. There was Heather, a woman their age, who had shaved her head to appear in traffic court. There was the Bradford kid, who would talk about cunnilingus at dinner in front of his parents. And poor Donny Lee, an enormous blind man who was the world's foremost authority on clover viruses. Spence listened carefully. He wondered if there were any sheep farmers left over there. He imagined the beauty Christine had been in this place where there were no average souls. What if he had known her then? Could he have competed with the Maori therapist?

Vera was asking him something.

"I said, if you could live anywhere, anywhere at all, where would you go?"

He thought about it. He had no answer for that one. He hadn't taught himself to think of place in those terms.

Vera looked at him sharply. She said, "You're saying you never get the urge to transplant? You never think about where you'd like to live?"

"Well, not like that." He wanted to suggest that this had more to do with money than imagination, but they were talking again. Vera favored England; Christine said

Italy. It seemed to Spence that their talk was a pretext for the spiritual abandonment of North America. It seemed to him that nobody was content to stay in any place known, any place where you had to live with your memory of limitations.

Vera said, "What about that swim?"

He tipped back in his chair. "You guys go ahead. I'll take a nap."

"A nap? Come on, Spence," Christine said, though not too coaxingly. He knew she wouldn't mind some time alone with her friend.

"Don't mind me. You two take your swim."

They changed and started down to the lake. Spence lay on the couch and listened to their voices, suddenly sharper and clearer as they entered the water. He heard them splash and laugh. The sun was softer through the screens and windows now. He listened to the voices fade, able to hear particular words and phrases. He could still hear them as he fell asleep.

The dream was memorable because he wasn't in it, and at first this was a relief. He didn't miss himself. But the lake was there, and the women — younger versions of Christine and Vera — and the soldiers. Dozens of men in uniform, lolling on the docks, eating and sleeping in tents or barracks just behind the trees. They moved slowly through the sunshine. Their presence was both courtly and disconcerting. They sat on the rocks and waved to the women as they paddled by in a red canoe. Spencer wanted to warn somebody, but he was not in the dream, and he didn't recognize its source. The uniforms moved in and out of the woods; the sheer number of them seemed to alter the quality of the sunshine.

He opened his eyes, feeling overwarm and anxious.

Nathalie was sitting on the edge of the couch, leaning back against his leg.

"Hey," he said. "You woke me up."

She gave him a brief, dull stare and turned to her book, a thick paperback with raised figures on the cover.

Spence lay like that for another minute or two, coming back to himself.

"What're you reading?"

"It's the second volume in a mole trilogy."

He closed his eyes and looked at her again.

"Moles? There's a trilogy about moles?"

"Yes. Their marriages and children and adventures above ground. Stuff like that. Also, there's a great flood. It's beautifully written."

In her sweatshirt and shorts Nathalie looked like a sulky Huck Finn, a bored tomboy who slouched and mumbled. But in the water, in her swimsuit, she was like a young dolphin, open-faced and friendly, willing to play. In the water she was buoyant and graceful, her female body revealed.

She leaned back on his legs and turned a page.

"Nathalie," he said. He felt awake now. He felt dangerously close to a revelation. "Nathalie, let me ask you something."

Slowly, as if she had forgotten he was in the room, she moved her head and looked at him.

"It's about your mother and me. I want to ask you something." He paused and continued: "What do you think we're doing? What do you think your mother and I are doing together?"

There was no reading her expression. Behind it there might be much or nothing.

"Well?" he said. "What about it?"

She waited another moment. Then she said, "I think it's private."

Spence nodded and pursed his lips. He could almost see Christine beaming with satisfaction at this answer.

"Besides," Nathalie said. "My mother's too old for you."

"Only six years."

She turned a page and made a face, as if this fact spoke for itself.

A song bird started up in a tree just outside, a clear and unambivalent trilling that struck him as wholly rare and unavailable to humans.

Nathalie cleared her throat and shifted her weight against him. He lay there and watched her turn a page, and then another.

That evening after supper Nathalie came out of her room with an old Chinese checker board and a box of marbles. Awakened from her bookish trance of the afternoon, she was now keen on gathering the others around the game. Spence threw down the dish towel and said, "Sure." Vera, ensconced in her own book, frowned but joined them, crosslegged around the board on the floor. Nathalie chattered happily while she assigned each player a different colored set of marbles. Spence began with black, but there weren't enough and four white ones were added to his troops.

"Let's go," he said. "Let's start." Though he couldn't have anticipated his reaction, the prospect of a contest excited him.

It began slowly, calmly. Spence knew that the game was won or lost in the opening moves. He made himself think ahead and behind. The women smiled and seemed to take their turns without much forethought. Spence told himself not to be fooled. They were in it to win. It pleased him to think of this simple competitive diversion coming down through the ages, from distant races and civilizations to this cottage on a northern lake. The premise was history itself. Armies massed on borders, territories to be taken by sheer will and numbers. No paper money or dice, no boardwalks or hotels. Direct and unsubtle.

But ten minutes into the battle Christine and Vera began nattering about female masturbation. Spence suspected they chose the topic to muddle his focus. Likewise, it struck him as strange and even hypocritical that Christine, who was adamant about keeping the straightforward reality of her sex life from Nathalie, would talk so breezily in front of her about the joys of self manipulation.

"Do we really have to discuss this now?" he said. "I mean, is it necessary to explore all the details at this stage of the game?"

"And what stage is that?" Christine said. She gazed at him cooly through a fringe of blonde hair that was paling to white rather than grey.

"All right, let's play," Vera said, and promptly jumped one of her green marbles half-way across the board in a single turn.

The talking stopped and they leaned closer to the conflict.

Nathalie, who had been chirping away to herself, became intent on her strategies and oblivious to the others, forgetting who had moved last. Though none of them had yet achieved a clear advantage, Spence felt that a breaking point was about to be reached, that the tides of colored marbles had converged at a kind of critical mass and shortly one player would gain a momentum that would be nearly impossible to catch. The women wore small, controlled smiles and took their turns without haste. He watched their hands move from the board to their laps or the floor. It was getting harder to visualize his own tactics: he kept forgetting that the white marbles were his and missed several opportunities to use them effectively. Turns were taken more quickly now; the playing field kept changing. Soon as he located a clear path an obstacle appeared or an opportunity vanished. He couldn't keep pace.

"Your move," Christine said.

Nathalie, on her knees and doubled over the board as though in pain, lifted her marble.

"No, it's Spencer's turn, Nat."

They watched the board and waited.

"Hurry up," Vera said.

Spence moved his tongue in his mouth and studied the board from angle to angle, end to end. Something was about to happen. The moment he made his move, the instant he committed himself, something would happen and he wouldn't be able to take it back.

"Come on, Spence. Let's go."

His hand hovered over the board and returned to his side.

"For heaven's sake," Vera said.

His other hand, the one he'd been leaning on, shot forward and the marbles jumped, rattled and swarmed across the board, some of them spilling to the floor and rolling around their feet and knees.

Nathalie shrieked and covered her eyes.

The women stared at him. Christine said, "I can't believe you did that."

"It was an accident! What — you think — ?"

Vera stood and stretched. Without comment she resumed her book in the corner chair. Nathalie went into her room and closed the door.

"Honestly," Spence said. He helped Christine find the marbles and return them to their box. "I was on the verge of breaking out. Why would I sabotage my own chances?"

"Tell me," she said. "Try to make me understand."

When the game was put away she suggested a walk down the road to the public beach. Vera told them to go ahead, she was going to bed early so she could get up tomorrow and take Christine's car on a day trip to visit relatives.

Outside, the air was cool, the darkness complete. Looking back, Spence could see Vera in the lit window, sitting motionlessly with her book. Her short sun-bleached hair was pushed behind her ear boyishly; her face was narrow and flinty, a projection of hard will and over-alertness.

He followed Christine down the dark path through the woods. When they reached the road, he said, "There's something about Vera. I wouldn't want her for an enemy."

There was a dim spot of moon behind muzzy clouds, like a dime at the bottom of the bay; he could barely make out the black shapes of trees around them.

He said, "I guess she has the right to be a little stern, after all that sickness."

"Oh, she's always been that way," Christine said.

They walked on, their shoes making dry muffled sounds on the unpaved surface. After a few minutes he could see the road, faintly aglow like chalk, and he imagined they were walking on another planet or through a valley on the moon.

He asked Christine if she would come to the cabin that night.

She considered and said, "I'll come in the morning."

They walked a little farther, and Spence said, "That won't work. I can't do that anymore."

He stopped and she stood beside him.

He said, "It's no good for you to sneak in at dawn so nobody notices. You think that's healthy? You think you're fooling anyone?"

"I'm protecting my daughter," she said.

"You're protecting yourself."

They stood and stared at the softly glowing road that curved into the cavernous dark.

"Maybe I am," she said. "But it's because I want to. It's what I want, and you can't change it."

He realized this was true. He understood the danger and futility of pretending it wasn't.

After awhile, he said, "Let's go back." But they stood there and peered into the night on both sides of them.

Spence lay on the quilts and read the book about the army of the future. What troubled him about it, what kept him reading, was the significant absence of characters in the narrative. There were names attached to figures, but no individuals with living traits. Spence couldn't decide if this was a literary defect or the deliberate and coldly accurate rendering of a particular vision of power. The soldiers, smiling boys and serious men, moved with one will, a sort of unconscious urgency that absorbed and overwhelmed the world before it. The army never fought, but it kept enlisting; it just got bigger. He dropped the book to the floor and mused on the cover representation of the Phelanian flag, which looked like a crusader's cross against a foreboding bank of clouds. The cross might be a crossroads, a legend of history as the sum of human decisions, all inevitable, all wrong — or it might be the abstracted figure of the phoenix, an individual rebirth founded on one small personal decision to start again.

He turned out the light and fell asleep listening for voices, for any sound at all, from the cottage next door.

The next day was hot and still. Vera didn't come back until the evening: suddenly she was sitting on a lawn chair between the cottage and cabin, looking tired but affected by her trip. Spence sat on the ground beside her while she talked about the aunts and cousins she had visited, memories that had been stirred, the faces that were lost and gone forever.

"Most of the younger ones have moved on, like me," she said. "Only a few of the older folks are left, and they don't seem connected to the past any more than I am."

She was trying to get at something, some part of herself, by talking about these things, as if she couldn't quite achieve a truly felt remembrance, as if her habitual mind thwarted the fullness of her own memory. She spoke of her sister, who had emigrated to Holland, and of her dead father, who had played semi-pro baseball for mining companies in tough northern towns, and of his pilgrimages down to big league stadiums in Cleveland and Philadelphia. Her voice was anxious but subdued, as though she were trying to rediscover the man with her talk but could only resurrect a shadowy outline, a wistful sketch.

Finally, she gave it up and went into the cottage.

In the silence, in the dark, through the filter of his sleep, he sensed a presence. Spence opened his eyes and held his breath. The cabin door had opened, and there was a footstep, and another. He rolled over. "Christine?"

"It's me. It's Vera."

He sat up; he didn't reach for the lamp.

"Vera," he said.

She sat on the bed. He could almost see her, a whitish shape in the close cabin darkness.

"What's going on? What's the matter?"

"I don't suppose . . ." she said, trailing off.

He sat a little straighter, straining to see.

She was sitting with her back to him, vaguely reclining against his raised knee, much like Nathalie had the other afternoon. She sat like that for two or three minutes, not long, and then slowly, almost stiffly, she stretched out beside him. Through the light flannel blanket he felt the form of her shoulder and thigh. She drew closer and released a long breath that felt warm on his neck. Spence lifted his hand and let his fingertips glide from the strap of her undershirt to her exposed clavicle and down the soft, thin fabric that covered her chest and ribs. His hand started to drift upward again and stopped. He lay on his back and waited. When he turned to speak she sat up and swung her feet to the floor. She sat as she had at the first, with her weight gently against his hip. Then she rose and disappeared toward the door. It opened and for a distinct instant he saw her silhouette against the starlit night. Then darkness again, the latch falling shut.

In the morning Spence wandered down to the water with half a notion of joining Christine before her morning circuit, only to meet Vera wading in. Christine and Nathalie splashed in circles a short distance from the dock. Vera said good morning and plunged, going under and surfacing between the others. Spence took some steps into the water and shivered. The sky held long, gray clouds. A few leaves floated on the dark water. He could have easily believed it was a month later. He went deeper and lifted his arms.

Christine called out, "Come on, Spence, we're swimming to the island. Can you do it?"

"The island," he said. "I think so."

Vera went ahead, swimming in determined jerks, spitting her breath.

"Come on," Christine called to him, and she leaned into her full stroke, unfolding herself like a shapely fish luxuriating in the element. Nathalie followed, equally delighted and at ease.

Spence took another step and started to swim. He heard them shouting and laughing, just ahead. Though he had no fear of the water, he understood that he was at a disadvantage. Already they were leaving him behind. He tried to settle into a rhythm. To reach the island he'd have to pace himself. The thing to do was concentrate on his own stroke and momentum. Forget the others.

He swam steadily and felt the land shrinking behind him, like a long memory. Certainly he was swimming back to some Silurian period of sheerly physical existence. The feeling came and went. He kept swimming. From the corner of his eye he saw Nathalie floating on her back like an otter. "Nat," he gasped, and immediately she slid under the water. She reappeared in front of him and went under again. Spence kept his stride, breathing and reaching, trying to ignore the crimp in his shoulders, the tightness in his chest.

Then something strange happened. He couldn't shake the impression that he was swimming in place. Somehow, by a trick of gravity or insidious undertow, he felt that for every deliberate stroke he took he lost one, stuck on a liquid treadmill between two shores. And yet the women were surging forward, diminishing into the distance. Faint snippets of talk and laughter fluttered back in their wake. He strove to kick free, to find the current that carried them along. But his renewed effort seemed to anchor him to the spot. The harder he worked, the more fixed he remained. Somewhere in the world a bell clanged, a brisk rolling call. Panic flooded his chest. The women were almost gone, as if disappearing into a different time, and it was hard to believe they hadn't waited for him.

When he couldn't see or hear them anymore he ceased to struggle.

Panic gave way to something like sadness. He floated on his back and felt the low, gray sky on his face, stomach and arms. The sky moved above him and he had the sensation of being towed backward, gently but purposefully, toward the shore he'd left behind. He closed his eyes and felt the shadows on his face; he sensed the green reflections of trees spreading on the water and the movement of figures along the shoreline. As the darkening current swung him closer he realized the troubled, voiceless forms of soldiers clad in soft gray fatigues drifting down from the forest, gathering silently near the water. He didn't know if they were the ghosts of men now living and already spent, or the prefigurement of a power yet to arrive. The lake held him there, close enough to remember or imagine them.

The lake held him at that distance.

MONK'S DREAM

A camper with the wrong kind of bumper stickers picks me up on the straight road between the Stanford shopping mall and the Linear Accelerator grounds.

Soon as I climb into the cab the driver asks, "VA hospital?"

No, I tell him, I'm headed up to the Skyline to see my buddy.

The driver, swollen like a balloon beneath his read sweat-shirt, nods and we take off. I look over my shoulder at the green knolls of lawn above the underground tunnels where atomic particles are raced and smashed and spun every which way for science's sake. I note the sun-bleached sign and the security gate where Jessica entered each day. I try to imagine the stupid hours she spent in a quonset hut typing for scientists who slept in their cars and wandered the grounds like metal patients waiting for the Big Idea. It's harder to remember the nights she spent alone or not alone while I played in the city with the band.

The driver reaches down to a little cooler on the floor and comes up with a plastic container full of chocolate pudding. He peels it open and ladles the pudding into his mouth with thumb and fingers. The container's empty before he changes gears again.

I mention the traffic, the weather. It's a perfectly golden California afternoon. The driver grunts and reaches for another pudding. We swing into the hills, up and down, hard turns through cool shadows of giant redwoods and firs. Robotic aliens on rocket bikes zoom around us. The driver reaches into the wind as if he'll grab the next one by his padded suit while the cycle zings away into oblivion.

Up on Skyline the camper brakes beside the trio of cockeyed mailboxes and lets me out in a cloud of yellow dust. Minus his original question the driver hasn't spoken a word. While I'm thanking him I notice at least six empty pudding containers on his lap and around his feet. He licks his fingers and slaps the truck into gear.

For a minute I stand there breathing the new air, dry and sweet, listening to the engine fade around the bend. My vision stretches over the rolling ochre hills, the occasional gnarled tree like an old soldier staring at caissons of clouds. I cross the pavement and step over the slack chain between posts planted on either side of the dirt road. The road winds down to Goose's trailer, snugged into the hollow between a wooded ridge and the old gray barn. His famous Chevy, a late 1940s model handed down from his grandfather, rests in the shadow of the barn. Everything but the car belongs to Goose's landlords, Frank and Howard, gay architects who live in a modern split-level on the far hill. If you know where to look you can spot a corner of their roof reflecting the afternoon sun. Otherwise, the trailer is the only dwelling in sight.

Shadows of two hawks make soft spirals on the hill.

From here, the trailer looks like a crazy space bug, the top hairy with antennae, the drab sides propped with jointed metal legs. No sign of Goose. The Chevy's back seat is strewn with books, cups, blankets. A jar lid of cigarette butts balanced on the transmission hump. At the trailer, I place one foot on the bent aluminum step and listen. I rap on the tinny door and it opens ghostily. Inside, stacked in the close gloom, tiers of tuners, speakers, tape decks, dubbing equipment. Rows of blinking lights and VU needles that flick in tiny lit windows as if measuring the silence.

But no Goose.

I lean out the door and call his name. A small, furtive wind raises dust devils around the car and rises to rustle the tall weeds and slender branches, a flowing *shhh . . .* that whispers over the hill into the blue. Then a racket of cracking branches along the ridge; the saplings part and Goose emerges sunburnt and dazed, his ears muffed in the biggest pair of headphones I've ever seen. He spots me, grins wide, and wades through the weeds.

"Look at this," he shouts, sweeping his hand. He looks like a satyr in surf shorts. "Hasn't rained up here in weeks. This isn't normal." And then, as an afterthought almost: "Hello, Vince. So you've come." His eyes focus inwardly on the sound between his ears. He touches one of the antennae rising like miniature antlers from the side of his head. "This is great. This is wonderful. I hope I'm getting this on tape."

He motions to follow him inside.

Veiled in secret shadows, the decks whir and blink. Goose slips out of the big phones and into a smaller pair wired to a tuner. He adjusts some knobs and grins.

"They've got Jack Benny on the Death Line. Yesterday they had Charles de Gaulle and Mama Cass."

"Death Line?"

"Interviews from the hereafter. They never say whether it's heaven or hell."

One of the decks clicks and its needles waver and drop. Goose lurches to snap out the cassette and enter a new one. At the cluttered kitchenette table he writes something in a notebook, puts a mark on the first cassette and drops it into a crate full of tapes.

"What is this, Goose? What is all this stuff?"

"This is The Experiment, Vince. This is what I've done with the last two months . . . Why I've missed so many practices."

He hoists a stein full of scummed coffee, gulps it, and settles on a stool. He looks like he's been living on locusts: his neck is red and unshaven, his thin sun-scorched hair stands up like it was glued in patches to his head. "It's all here, Vince. The whole mad civilization that comes in on the airwaves. I'm getting all of it. Do you realize the investment I've made in time and materials? Weeks and weeks of tape. An average of fifteen of every twenty-four hours. News, music of every hue, commentary all over the ideological road. Have you listened to talk radio lately? Hundreds of little Hitlers with their own shows. Amazing."

He shakes his head and glugs the cold coffee.

"So what? What's the point?"

"Point? Look, I'm taping six different channels, FM and AM, even as we speak. End of the week I sit down and splice the best, which is often the worst, into half-a-dozen cassettes. I can do that. Splice and dub. It's a cinch."

I shrug and raise my palms.

"Vince, I thought sure you'd get it. You, of all earthly souls. See, what I'm making here is history. Real history out of post-history. We're inhaling the air of Plato, Hume, and Nietzsche and exhaling the air of Elvis, Pepsi, and the Japanese stock exchange, which is the air of nothing. Or nearly nothing. But I'm getting it the only place it can be got, on sound tape. In sound."

"But why? Why bother?"

"Because this is all that's left. Sounds on the air. And I've discovered my calling at last. To render the airwaves. Deep in the most commercial of programming, embedded in the literal format, is the meaning that lights up for the sheerest instant. I'm doing it because it's the last meaningful work to be finished. He who hath ears, Vince. He who hath ears."

He drains the coffee and grins through the rosy brown mask of his sunburn.

It's possible that he's lost it. It's just possible that Goose has left us for cartoon land, a never-ending Saturday morning loony tune in his head. But when I laugh, he laughs.

"Jesus, I don't know," I say, and we keep laughing, both of us looking at the crate full of tapes.

"It's the only real record of the fading world," he says. "Like glyphs on the sphinx. Full of secrets. Reads the same in either direction. It's in the tapes. I'll boil them down to maybe ten solid hours of the strangest and truest and mail them out to radio stations for rebroadcast, or museums and universities, anyone who'll listen. There may even be money in this."

"I don't know, Goose," I say, my tone sobering.

Another deck shuts down and he scrambles to reload. He writes in the notebook, marks the finished cassette, and tosses it into the crate.

"Every tape is a display case of emotions and ideas that won't exist in another twenty years. Like those Victorian display cases stocked with extinct birds. But in sound."

He means it. I can see this is important to him. This is what Goose has instead of romance or money. The same Goose who suffered through Hermeneutics back in seminary, who up and left in the middle of the school year. It wasn't a case of following him, not exactly. Jessica and I had our reasons, the music being a big one. But sometimes it seems that this Goose is not the same one I knew in Philadelphia.

He says, "We've lost the world of images, Vince. The old optics have been ruined for this generation by profane video. But we still have sound. Don't forget it. Sound preceded light and sound will save you when all's said and done."

This is not what I hitchhiked up the mountain to hear. This is not what I thought I needed.

"What's that face?" he says. "There's that Vince face."

"Maybe we should just have a beer or something. Have a beer and put some Gerry Mulligan on the stereo."

He stands with the headphones around his neck, the wire leashing him to the dark machinery. Then he takes them off and says, "Right. We need air."

Outside, we lean on the Chevy. A dry wind ruffles the weeds, pushes the silence around. I sense the ocean to the west; to the east the mad traffic that ebbs and flows. Earth time running beside human time, above and below. Separate meanings that sometimes intersect, like knowledge and belief. The former, we know, exists in gradients. But a little belief is nothing like a modicum of knowledge. A little belief is a germ, a seed. A little knowledge is a nut without a bolt. Merely incomplete.

"What's Vince thinking?"

"He's thinking what he should have thought in seminary."

Goose reaches into the front seat for his cigarettes and offers me one. I tell him no thanks, I quit. He sighs, as if he's heard that one before.

"Caffeine and cancer sticks," he says. "They're killers. But heaven hates a drunkard and a whoremonger, and I'm neither of those."

His voice is soft and bemused now. The metal of the old car is warm and solid like desert bone. I believe I could stretch on the corroded roof and sleep through the millennium.

"Ever have second thoughts about seminary, Vince?"

"I have second thoughts about everything. That's my problem."

He asks me this question every month or so, and my answer always changes. But I know that I'm no better on the trombone than I was with the books. All this change and movement and fair weather have given me nearly zip in the count of secular advantages.

"Time to eat," Goose says, pushing off the fender he's been leaning on. "I'll make you the best salad you ever had, Vince. A salad to put hair on your heart. An epic salad. The salad from those days everybody talks about."

He's happy and animated again, still talking salad as he steps inside the trailer. The bent door bangs open and out he comes with a large silvery bowl like a hubcap under his arm. I climb onto the stout hood of the Chevy and watch Goose crouch in his garden, a plot as wide and long as the trailer.

"Growing food and making tapes," he calls out in his best pulpit voice. "The delicious extremes of the 20th Century."

"It can't go on forever."

"We can expect a frost any night now," he says cheerfully.

The greens and bulbous vegetables plop in the silver bowl. Goose straightens, pushes his fist into the small of his back. "Give me a minute," he says. "I'll bring supper out."

"Can I help?"

"Naw, in my kitchen I'm supreme."

The afternoon has cooled toward evening. A chalk smudge of moon shows behind the paling blue.

Goose comes out balancing a tray stacked with bowls and cups. He does an ungainly dance across the dirt and weeds to the car. I slide off the hood and hold the tray while he goes around to the trunk, opens it, whips out a small lavender cloth. He shuts the trunk, spreads the cloth on it and motions for the bowls of food. There's salad drenched in honey dressing, cheese, and a loaf of partially frozen brown bread.

"You made this? Where'd you learn to make bread?"

"Not in seminary," he says.

He pours tea from a squat Aztec-type pot. Delicate spouts of steam purl up from the cups. The salad is good as promised. I ask what's in it.

"Can't you tell?"

I eat fast and wash it down with three or four cups of strong Chinese tea. Chunk of bread in hand, Goose points to the western slope. A young doe is making her way down it like she's wandered out of the sky. She chooses careful steps and at one point turns her face toward our voices.

We talk about the band. I tell him the guys are sore about the practices he's missed.

He nods and says, "That's why I don't have a phone here. I miss some action, sure, but it saves me from a lot of stress."

"Nevertheless, sooner or later they'll get fed up."

"Yass, yass," he says softly.

"I'll tell you something, Goose. I have a feeling about the band, about the music in general. I can't put my finger on it, but I'm not playing like I used to. It's getting away from me. I can't feel it. I can't hear it in my head like before. I have a hunch: when I'm done with the band I'll be through with the music."

Goose listens and releases a long breath.

"Don't funk yourself," he says. "All you have to do is keep going for awhile. Play what you know. You'll do all right."

The dark and cold have crept down from the hills. The trailer reflects the dying light like wreckage on the moon. We stack the supper things on the tray and I carry it through the wet grass. Inside, Goose finds the light and I leave the tray beside the small sink. He kneels beside the tape decks and makes fine adjustments.

With his back to me, Goose says, "I have a feeling about the band, too. Between us, I may not be around much longer."

Surprised, I say, "Nobody would blame you if you found a better band."

"It's not just that." He turns to another deck; his eyes come up to mine. "Vince, I wish I could tell you what I've learned listening to these tapes, just cruising the radio dials. I've heard it all, and now I'm waiting for the numbers to align."

"The numbers?"

"The digits on the tape counters. When they all come up 999 at more or less the same moment." His voice runs low, excited. "Think about it. What are the odds for that kind of synchronicity? When it happens, would you dare call it chance? Those old magic numbers. You know'em, Vince. You know. And remember. 999 is 666 upside down."

I put a thoughtful look on my face and nod. "But what has that got to do with the tapes?"

"What? I'm telling you! Soon as the counters jibe, the experiment stops. At a perfectly random alignment the machine shuts down. It's jazz, Vince. You and I know that the only perfect moment is the perfectly random one, the randomness of its perfection and vice versa. We know. The numbers come up, the machine shuts down. That's all."

"And?"

"And I sell this hardware, buy some reliable transportation and clear out. I think. I don't have any hard plans, but anything is possible. That's the beauty of it. Anything is possible. Besides, Frank and Howard keep threatening to sell."

"But where would you go? East? You wouldn't go back east, would you?"

"East, maybe. Or north. Like I said, I'm not making concrete plans. I don't want to jinx my trajectory by making it too conscious."

We blink at the dirty dishes as though their incidental configuration posed the riddle of the pyramids, the conundrum of the ages.

"You know, Vince, you were good at theology. You had an inspired knack."

I ask him if he remembers Jessica. They met once or twice in Philadelphia, one or twice out here.

"I remember she was quiet," he says. "I remember thinking she knew more about music than she let on. She knew a lot of things, but she didn't want to talk."

A deck shuts down with a dry belch. Goose scrambles to feed it a fresh cassette. Around us, the tiny wheels turn like inexorable time, an ontology of sounds and signs that cannot be dismissed, whether we hear them or not. I step back into the cramped bedroom at the end of the trailer, a space just big enough for the sleeping bag laid out amid shapeless piles of clothes. I lie down on the bag and fold my hands over my stomach. The darkness breathes lightly, full of hidden signals.

Goose calls back, "Vince, you know what we should have been? We should have been barbers. Now there's a vocation. It's not for everyone. You have to understand people. You have to know what it means to have a body in the chair."

I listen on the brink of sleep, that impersonal awareness that comes with not caring, or at least not caring enough to talk about it.

"Yass, we'd have us a little shop in downtown San José. We'd cater to the geezer market. We'd jammer with the old boys about inflation and aphids. We'd wear doubleknit trousers and soft shoes. Hot empty afternoons we'd sit back in those leather thrones and sip RC Cola and listen to Bobby Darren on the radio and stare at the *Field & Stream* pictures on the wall. Think about it . . ."

And I do, I think about those hot afternoons and that little shop with an old fan rattling in the corner, back issues or *Argosy* and *Popular Mechanics* yellowing on the table. Outside, drowsy downtown streets, the rumble of a motor receding deeper into the dream . . .

I sit up in the close, ticking dark. Silence talking to silence. I stumble forward to the decks and amps. "Goose?"

"Out here."

Open the door and step into the night. Shiver and look up at the moon, cold and small in its new winter incarnation. Goose stands a few yards away staring down the dirt lane, as if someone he knows will soon walk toward us.

"When I come out here," he says, "after making tapes, there's always a moment, a split instant, when I hear something."

"What do you hear?"

He shrugs. "What I hear is a premonition of sound or a fading vibration, never the whole thing beginning and ending."

I wait and keep my silence, as if I might hear it too.

"If it's out there, I'll get it on tape sooner or later. God's own theme song, Vince. If I can't make it up or play it, I'll pull it out of the airwaves."

"I believe you."

An animal cry carries down from the hill like someone in pain playing an ancient saw. Neither yap nor yowl, it falls with slow expressiveness, other-worldly, with a resonance that lingers, an afterimage that fairly glows.

"Anyhow," Goose says, "you might as well stay the night. You can sleep where you were and I'll sack out in the car. I've been sleeping there lately."

Inside, he finishes his workday by putting new cassettes in the machines to turn off automatically when they run out. He says good night and takes his cigarettes and a gas camp lantern out to the Chevy. I stand at the door and watch his light bob through the dark and fill the cavernous old car, a greenish dome beneath frozen stars. He props his stockinged feet on the dash. One hand supports an open book. The other, with lit cigarette, comes up and turns a page.

I hit the lights in the trailer and feel my way back to the sleeping bag. Lying there, I can see the tape decks blinking down the night corridors like small towns in Wyoming, Nebraska, Ohio. The damp cold penetrates the floor. Within seconds of each other the machines shut down — clack, clack, clack — their lights gone out.

The sleepy void gives way to the clatter of removed goings-on. Around the diminishing edges of a dream men are at work. No voices, only the rasp of saws, tools clanking against tools. Steady fusillades of hammering.

I wriggle out of the bag in the windowless gloom, my breath rising in steam. I shiver to the bright fore-end of the trailer to peer through the frosted window over the sink. I rub the pane with my palm and look again. A fine new snow, inviting as food, covers the slope. Sky like polished chrome against a fringe of green trees. And six or seven sets of footprints lead down the hill toward the barn. The trailer door bangs open and Goose shuffles in hugging a faded Indian blanket over his head and shoulders.

"Hoo! Will you look at this," he says, pushing close to the window.

The glass sweats and clears before our focused breath. Something's moving out there on the snow. A strange new god, a convoluted dragon wobbling on unsteady legs. Or the skeletal hull of a Norse ship with pterodactyl wings, staggering over the thin new snow like it was looking for its creator. And then we see the men beneath it, bearing it along, men of medium height, fair, with blonde whiskers and ruddy cheeks. Slowly, lovingly, they lay their burden down. A few mop their brows with orange or blue bandanas. They wear holstered tools or carry rolled charts in their hands. None of them speak as they move in and out of our vision.

"What is it? What's going on?"

"It's the club. Frank and Howard's club. Every Sunday they come out of the city and down from the mountain like the Nephilim."

"But what's that they're building?"

"Airplane. They're building an airplane," he says, grinning wildly, as though this fact had just occurred to him.

"An airplane? Out of what?"

"Nuts and bolts. Whatever it takes, I guess. Frank says they'll be flying by spring."

The sun sings on the white hills. I try to remember the last time I saw snow. Several of the men take off their boots and step barefoot through it. Their tanned ankles flash like brass as they haul and fit the jointed struts to their flying machine. A perfectly bald and square-shouldered man in a singlet and torn shorts stands aside from the others, surveying their progress. He has a broad golden moustache and the morning sun bronzes his head like a helmet. His eyes are pale blue, hopeless and concentrated, lost to all causes but the one at hand. On silent cue he steps into the ranks and a dozen bare muscled arms lift the framework: it rises and wavers as though they'll toss it into the sun.

Goose shifts beneath his blanket.

"Time to get to work. I should get the tapes rolling."

But we lean closer to the window, shoulder to shoulder, our faces near the glass, waiting for that one among them who would speak first.

CITY OF GOD

Hitting town on the Harmonic Convergence Sunday, the tenth anniversary of Elvis Presley's passing, and three years exactly since I've seen my wife. Ex-wife. All on the same Sunday. When I left California my friends were skeptical, even worried. They warned that I wouldn't be tolerated in the workaday east. They said I'd turn white and overdose on meaning. But the signs pointed in this direction and after Elko I knew I was moving toward this city in upstate New York where I was born thirty-three years ago, where my father is buried, where my wife — ex-wife — is an administrator at the university. I have no intentions other than to visit my father's grave, which I have never seen.

And it's here. Feel it. Thick and humid, in the shabby motels and used-tire dumps. The boxy frame houses with feral dogs sleeping on the stoops. My lost home, God help me, my holy source.

The road loops downward into the hot belly of town, carrying my car like a steel ball in the coiled track of a child's toy. Crumbling churches and Gothic parking garages, the seedy midtown Sheraton, everything a gray shimmer that seems to slide to one side like soft dirty butter.

For the first time in a dozen states I turn off the radio. I want to take it all in, fill my eye, locate frequency. I chant the names of trees and presidents, trying to beg some magic. The streets are strangely empty, but not to worry. All things meet in the amplitude of time if not the glory of passion. Don't I know that? I'm aiming for that particular intersection of personal history and larger time, that locus where final meaning will shed its light. Might be my father's grave or the park where Carol and I got engaged. I know this is the time and place for fate to kiss my lips. Like those freaks at Mount Shasta or Graceland, I don't laugh at anyone. I took to signing in at motels as Larry Archaeopteryx and nobody even asked.

Exit and shift. Touch the stick of sandalwood on the dash. Down a street of heaved pavement and big shaggy trees like soiled mammoths. Did anybody ever live in these houses? Did real boys toss basketballs through the rusted rims on leaning garages? Their ghosts fill the back seat and passenger side, ghosts of laughing city kids in their spiritual summer clothes.

I turn and turn again; the houses give way to gutted service stations and starving body shops with twisted wrecks in front. Razed foundations like Celtic ruins, a red Pegasus on its back in the broken glass and weeds. Turn again, climb a ramp that routes me through a maze of hulking fuel tanks with little cat-walks on top. The tanks are blasts of white heat against a blindingly blue sky. I need directions. I need a drink.

The road cuts straight through a plateau of crushed gravel, no grass or green at all, just a few shacks and derrick-like contraptions in the distance. Stretches of barbed wire and suddenly, praise be, a beer sign blinking colorlessly in a window, a faint dry pulse against the midday sun.

I turn in and the car balks, dies chugging. Easy, I say, patting the dash. We're not there yet. Not quite.

Stone crunches underfoot to the door. Inside it's a little cooler and dark. Empty but for the boy in white T-shirt working behind the bar. He straightens and pushes the pale, wetted hair from his eyes. Before I speak he pulls tap and sets a full one before me.

"Hot," I say.

"Some like it," he replies, without a trace of smartass.

The beer is cold and I drink it fast. It makes the base of my cranium creak on its stem. The road vibration in my back turns into a long delicious shiver. When I find my father's grave I will take off my shoes and stand barefoot in the grass, in the cool blowing shadows of cemetery trees. I'll touch his name with my finger and know it was worth every mile and crummy truckstop.

I raise my glass. "One more of these."

While he draws it the kid talks. He says, "You're from out of state."

"What makes you think so?"

"You got that look. Plus, I seen your plates."

He sets the glass between my hands and folds his arms. He has all the time in the world.

"A week ago I was on the last beach," I tell him. "Just a week ago I was lying on the sand without a thought in my head. That's why I went and that's why I left."

"Sounds nice," he says. "Ever been this way before?"

I tell him I did two years in medical school way back when. He nods, not very much impressed. He says, "Two years and you quit. How come?"

"Burn out and hepatitis. Worked too hard down in animal research. When I got better I took off for the coast. Been there since."

"The beach," he says.

"That's it."

He produces a rag from under the counter and presses it to the back of his neck.

"Listen," I say, "would you believe me if I told you that my wife, my ex-wife, lives beside the cemetery where my father's buried? It's a fact. She owns a condo beside that big cemetery near the university. She's almost a dean in the engineering school."

The boy looks over his shoulder. "What's not to believe?" he says.

"I haven't seen her in years and I've never seen my father's grave. Think about it. I'll be standing at his marker and when I look up I'll see her building in the distance. What do you make of that?"

He turns away. "Let's have some music," he says. He reaches up to a radio. It's Elvis doing the spoken part from *Are You Lonesome Tonight?* The part where he says all the world is a stage and each must act his part.

"That's all they've been playing for days," the boy says.

"Think of every song as a prayer," I tell him. "Tell yourself that every song on the radio goes up like a prayer. If that's what you make it, that's what it is."

"I'll keep that in mind," he says. He works his way down the bar, wiping it with the rag. Without looking at me, he says, "How you going to find that grave if you've never seen it before?"

I empty the glass and step off the stool.

"It's been described to me," I say.

What I don't tell him is that I dreamed this grave fast asleep in the chair of an Elko motel room, the television blaring. I dreamed a tremendous vault, an embroidered globe poised on four silver monkeys, the monkeys atop pillars like barber poles braced in turn upon four jeweled elephants on a tomb of gold. And the tomb was an ancient ship, a galleon without sails. It was a baroque city full of music, a hundred thousand violins and kazoos.

The boy says, "Well, good luck anyhow. Stay cool."

I peel a bill from the roll in my shirt pocket. The glass finger of remedy I've been carrying since San Francisco falls to the counter and rolls. Perfect finger, tapered like a woman's. The boy eyes it but says nothing as I slip it back into my shirt.

At the door I turn and wave. He stands there, the money untouched on the bar.

I push out to the lot, through the heat over parched

gravel. Music leaks from the tavern. I get in the car and slam the door. Behind the wheel it doesn't sound like anything, not even silence.

Back on the arterial I glance at the fuel gauge, forgetting it broke in Illinois. I take the glass finger from my pocket and shake it, the tiny pellets click like beads. My last job in San Francisco was at the zoo, in the primate cages. Feeding and cleaning. Mostly cleaning. Worked with a young woman who was overjoyed with apes. She loved their eccentricities, their long faces full of yearning and innocence. She was in love with the hyperactive rhesus, the curmudgeonly baboon. This woman was all glow and muscle, like a beautiful animal herself. She'd laugh, chasing monkey flap with high-pressure water guns. When the fever came back she noticed me taking the remedy. She admired the finger and mentioned it until I felt obliged to make it a gift. But I didn't. Let her earn it, I thought. And this woman, this beauty, who once pleased and amazed me by doing a perfect handstand in the parking lot, she faded with the primates, with the crazy laughter of summer. Driving across the country I wondered if I hadn't made a mistake, if I shouldn't have stayed in her world. For her, the zoo was another sort of beach; a less final one. Her intention was positive, her forms and expressions were shapely, but I decided that a quasi-beach was no better than the bedlam city and possibly worse in the medium run.

Floating in over the downtown roofs; off in the haze Winged Mercury balances on the peak of an ancient savings bank. He's green and patchy like a beached salmon decomposing under the sun. My sign shimmers up and the exit drops me fast off the loop, back into the city's rusted gut. Down here in the hollows, among the concrete abutments and skeletal trestles, the light is like algae on the windshield. I'm the lone car at the intersection; I get the signal and follow the arrows toward the university, climbing again, past the parking lots and the hospital, up into the sunshine, among the fast food restaurants and sundry shops edging the campus.

Park and set the brake. Out in the heat and glare, breathing deep. I remember this. I've been here before with Carol. We ate pizza right across the street.

No pedestrians, no traffic. A few cars parked at meters. Where is everybody? The cemetery is a good mile or two from here, but I want to see this. I want to walk through what I remember.

Ticking off the familiar: same barber shop and burger joint. Same battered phone booth at the corner. I step inside to center myself. A little glass cubicle for looking out, for watching the sharks. Today there's nothing to see and the booth is stifling. Before I can stop myself I put money in the slot. It's an old rotary phone that swallows my coin like it's the one it's been waiting for all week. The dial grinds and clicks. The voice makes me jump. What city? it asks. For a moment I can't remember. For a moment my brain inside this booth is a city unto itself, full of self-generating data and sad Christmas lights. What city? it asks again. This one, I say and the phone says, Go ahead. I say the name and the numbers come fast; I sing them out while my finger finds them on the dial. Grind and click. Grind and click.

It's ringing. My God, it's ringing. Don't do it, Larry. Get out of here. Run. It's ringing and I'm falling backward through a canyon of time, falling through epochs and eons, through wars and droughts and bad weekends.

What if she answered in the old affectionate manner? What if she said, "Hi Lango —" Her pet name for me, short for Langur monkey from when I worked with them in the labs. What if she hangs up in my face?

I count the fifth ring with something like relief, and just as I move the receiver toward the hook her voice comes through — clear, imperative.

"It's me," I say.

A blue buzzing silence. All the ions in the universe streaming between our two ears. All the bones of extinction locked in deep subterranean frost.

"Larry?" she says. I see her close her eyes, press her fingertips to her forehead.

"That's right. How are you, Carol?"

"Larry, you're not in town, are you?"

"I am. I came to see Pop. His grave."

"Why?"

"I drove here from California. It's about time, don't you think? I think this is the time."

Hiss of the void. Sound of nothing.

"I thought we might have a coffee or something. I thought now might be the time for a quick visit. Just a quick one."

More dead space. More nothing.

"I'll be back on the road by evening, I promise."

I'm sweating in here, my head against the smudged glass. I can't breathe or see out. One more word might lose her.

"All right," she says. "All right. Just this once. But stay where you are. I'll meet you."

I tell her the street and she agrees to be here in half an hour. For a minute I lean on the phone, catching my breath. Back in Nebraska, just outside of Lincoln, I stopped at a boarded-up gas station to call the talk show DJ I'd been listening to all night. The glass was shattered but the phone worked, and I stood in the dark with the occasional big rig blasting down the highway and I told this man, this stranger on the radio, about the comings and goings of my life. He asked me why I left the coast. I told him, "Skinheads came trick-or-treating through my building on Christmas Eve. Next day I was attacked by a Doberman in a sweater. All my neighbors have been shot at least once." He listened and said, "Don't you think you're being negative?" I laughed and cursed him. I told him I had a gun in my trunk and I was on my way to plug the president. I dared him and the whole FBI to find me on this road, in this long long night.

Out of the booth and walking, tripping on the seams in the concrete like a drunk. Third time around the block she's at the corner. She smiles behind unlikely wraparound sunglasses. I kiss her cheek and she steps back.

"I thought we'd get a quick drink down the street," she says.

I can see she's dressed for action other than mine: black heels and skirt and a thin summer jacket. Plainly, I'm about to get the dust-off.

"I'm short on time myself," I tell her. "Why don't we just take a walk?"

She turns the dark glasses on me, hesitates, and says,

"If that's what you want."

Who put her into this hard woman's get-up? Who gave her the asymmetrical haircut and the snaky earrings? If I asked, she'd say, You. You did.

We walk.

Carol moves calmly, exact measure in her stride. She asks polite questions, as though she's interviewing me for a position that's already been filled. She's timing this, every word and gesture subtracted from the clock. I have fifteen or twenty minutes and this one will be history, like the rest.

"So you're looking for your father," she says.

"I owe him that much. You never tracked him down? You live so close."

She stops and turns her head slowly, those damn glasses again. "How do you know where I live?" she says.

"What? What are you talking about? I've always known. You sent mail, I wrote back. What do you mean?"

"You haven't been calling me, have you?"

"Calling you?"

"My phone keeps ringing. Somebody leaves creepy messages on my machine."

The heat comes off the sidewalk. There's a chemical smell like sweat and bad eggs on the town.

"Carol, come on. I just got here."

"That's right," she says, walking on.

Was a time we were one name and address, and this heartened me. Now I understand why she gave it back, and not gave it back so much as got out from under, shifted a weight. Given the choice, I might do the same.

We walk down a long hill, between diners and overgrown lots and dark video arcades with strange sounds spilling into the street. She asks about my trip. She seems surprised I haven't lost the car along with everything else.

"Did you see anything interesting on the way?" she asks. "You must have done some sightseeing. I know you go the back roads and take your time. What did you see out there?"

These are trick questions. My answers are accordingly terse. If I start to tell it, it'll come out wrong, all wrong. It will fill up the present and sweep us under.

"It's not like you not to have stories, Larry. You always had a good one up your sleeve."

"I just came to see the grave. I'm not here to make any impressions."

"Strange," she says. "That doesn't sound like you."

Our pace slackens. We look at each other. She smiles behind her sunglasses and shrugs. We walk on with the clock ticking. I can hear it. I feel the weight of the endless silence, the negative vacuum she's learned to live inside. And then, despite myself and in the face of that shining blankness and unflappable void, I start to tell her about a roadhouse in New Mexico where I shot billiards with some kind of Navajo-Chinese, a squat fellah hipster with pigtails and capped teeth. He wore frayed lavender trousers and padded around the table on flat bare feet like tortillas. Between shots he leaned his face against my chest and cried in a high cracked voice, *We are breast-fed babies and cannot help ourselves.* He followed me to the bar and said it again. *We are breast-fed babies and cannot help ourselves.* The he laughed like a jungle bird and sang a short chorus in an abrupt and guttural tongue. Later, in the parking lot, he found me getting into my car. A full moon hovered over the wire fence. He put a scarab ring in my palm and closed my fist on it. When I tried to return it he scowled and shook his head. I got in the car and drove off, the moon following in the rearview like his face.

"Where is it now? Do you have the ring?"

"I didn't like the way it bumped around in my shirt pocket. I could feel the weight of it on my chest. Back on the interstate I rolled the window and threw it out."

"It might have been worth something," she says.

"Maybe, but I didn't want its karma following me across the map."

Carol listens with an interested and satisfied expression. It's not the whole story but I've given her what she wants. Damn me, I've put out a line of fool talk that tells her exactly the thing. She walks ahead enveloped in triumphant silence, supported on pure negativity, that knowledge which is the literal definition of me and which I am powerless to disprove by any means.

"I know what you're thinking," I say. "Why do you do it? Why do you make me talk?"

"Oh, I like that," she says. "As if I ever made you do anything. I refuse the blame," she says, "for what happens to you or the way you think. It's just you, Larry. You're the only person living your life."

I'm still thinking about that one when the air between us fills with a high and goofy cry, a sound that seems to ripple over the blank sidewalks. We cross the street and look down an alley between a laundromat and a donut shop. A black guy in psychedelic robes and a fez squeezes a nasal wail from a saxophone so small it looks like a toy.

His purple cheeks balloon as he fingers the instrument, bouncing his sound between the brick walls. The diminutive sax, intricate and golden, looks like a calibrated angel wing, a sacred artifact. He dips it in our direction and does a little dance.

"Did you see that?"

Carol moves on, walking fast. I hurry to catch up and she stares straight ahead through the dark glasses. She knows I'm excited and encouraged over something that's probably not there.

"Let's go," she says. "I'm running out of time."

We head back toward the street where I'm parked. It's now or never, so I ask her, with all the wrong words and inflections, with tics and giveaways that fit the file she put together on me long ago — I ask her if she will go with me, if she'll help me find my father's grave.

For the first time she takes the glasses off, reveals the unwavering blue of her eyes.

"You want me to help you," she says. "You want me to look around that cemetery with you."

We look at each other for a long, arid moment. A moment that hangs a balance or signifies nothing at all, like a desert crossroads.

"That's it. Why not? You live right next door."

She turns and takes big angry steps in her small black shoes. She says, "You take the cake, Larry. Did you know that? You really take the prize."

"Jesus, this is my father. You knew him. He was good to you."

"I don't want anything to do with it," she says. "You're trying to involve my feelings and I refuse to take responsibility. You're trying to involve me with the fact that you didn't make his funeral, that he died in the first place."

She means that she turned me down when I asked for airfare to come back for the burial. The fact that my father died and I was too broke to fly home was none of her doing. She's saying it had nothing to do with her life.

In a clear, raised voice I say, "I've come a long way for this. I've spent all my money and traveled hard to make an honorable finish."

She puts the glasses back on, two little whorls of fire.

"All right," she says, "but this is it. Understand? This is the end. We'll take my car and make it fast. And remember," she says. "Remember what I said."

A fierce blue heat comes off the parking lot and it hurts to look at the cars. There's a sound of air conditioners laboring in the windows of the two condo buildings.

"Which one is yours?" I ask. "Where's your apartment?"

"Never mind. Let's get this over with."

We take a few steeps and my legs go spongy, my head fills with popping lights. The sun pounds down on everything.

"What is it?" she says. "What's the matter?"

I lean on the nearest car and take the remedy from my pocket. The finger is stoppered with a tiny cap. I fill the cap with white pellets and knock them back. Carol stares at me suspiciously.

"What's all that about?"

"Nothing. I'm fine."

She frowns and points. "The cemetery is this way," she says, and she starts to walk. She's heard everything I have to say. But what if I got down on my knees in this parking lot and told her what I've seen, the skull-shaped cloud over Utah, the low-flying eagle with something in its talons that looked like a tiny frantic man. And somewhere in the desert off Route 285 a pack of dogs pulled down a deer on the run, a kicking gazelle surrounded and sucked into the infernal machine. There was nobody but me to see it and I got off the road and out of my car and walked a mile, maybe more, until I had the right words in my heart, and I knelt in the warm sand and prayed for all the torn and savaged lives, the lives succumbed to fear and darkness. I prayed for my lost wife, alone or not alone in the city of her choice, subject to the same wolves, the same inhuman grind, the vicious gears eating up and spitting out . . .

"Let's get this show on the road," she says.

We cross the sticky tar and cut behind the second building. She leads me through a broken wooden gate, along a winding path between overgrown bushes and patches of white wildflowers. We stop on the narrow cindered road that runs to the first grave rows.

"Where do you want to begin?" she says.

I motion at a valley of marble pillars below a ridge of shade trees. Carol clips ahead in her back heels, her black skirt and glasses, like a celebrity mourner who came to interment services for someone she didn't know. She leads me among the salmon-colored markers, she marches over the shadows of venerable cedars and pine. There's a coolness in here the season can't touch.

"Is this the place?" she says. She pauses, perusing the legends on stone. "He wouldn't be here, would he?"

"A little farther, I think. Down there."

We move on, among larger, stranger monuments. Buddhist stupas and crosses with hands. A sculpted lion's head with rock and roll lyrics between its fangs. Carol takes off her glasses and looks around.

"What is this?" she says. "Who'd bury their dead in a place like this?"

"Come one," I say, and I take the lead down the hill, our ankles awash in dry brown leaves. At the bottom Carol stops to brush bits of twig from her stockings. We're surrounded by massive vaults, canopies of trees, silence upon silence. I know not to speak. For once I'm not even tempted. We wander past a towering white elk and a black granite urn in the coils of a winged snake. Around the next bend the vessel of my dream will reveal itself, will justify my reason and redeem my past.

We walk around a tomb with stained-glass windows and a poem about tigers and lambs engraved beneath the names.

Carol leans closer to read the inscriptions.

"Children are buried here," she says.

She follows me up the opposite slope.

"Let's just sit awhile," I say. "Let's just rest for a minute."

We sit on the dry grass. We're listening for what comes next. We're watching for the fair wind that will point us toward my father's grave. It's just ahead. We're almost there.

"Let me kiss you," I say.

She shakes her head but I do it anyway. She squeezes my hand and says something. I draw her closer; we slide a little on the grass. I want to tell her, Hold tight, time is running out. I want to say, After this there's nothing left of us. We kiss and slide a little farther, her skirt pushing up; we slide slowly down toward the pillars and stones until she grasps my hands and mouths a hard *No!*

"Wait a minute. Don't worry," I say. "Just a minute."

But she clambers up the hill, reaching back for her shoe. I try to follow and slip to my hands, watching as she gropes for balance and jams the glasses back on.

"Carol?"

"Just quit. Leave it."

I reach for a leaf in her hair and she pushes my hand away.

"That was stupid," she says.

She's right. If I find the grave now, what will it mean with what's going on in me? I feel for the finger in my pocket. Gone. Between here and the tomb.

"I didn't mean anything," I say.

"Right."

I sit at the top of the hill and rest my head on my knees. I can hear everything. The ghost of every sound, the echo of every hope and brave idea.

Above and behind me, she says, "I'm going now, Larry. I'm going back now." She waits awhile. "Goodbye then," she says.

I can hear her shadow moving through the grass. After a short distance she stops. Next she'll say, "If I were you I wouldn't waste my time here. I'd cut my losses and find a home." Or, "Give yourself a break, Larry. Don't get caught up in the signs."

But she doesn't speak and behind her I can hear the whispers of names, small wings in the trees. She turns and starts again. I listen to her walk through the late summer grass and dead leaves. I picture what she is and was, what I knew and the illusion of that knowledge. I picture thin ankles and blonde hair with a premature streak of grey. I hear her walking out of memory and I keep my eyes on the grass because when she steps out of this place she'll be more than gone, she'll be as if she never was.

The car starts with a thunking cough and I gun it to the skyway with wrenching shifts. The radio's giving me *Mystery Train* and the maps fly around in the back seat.

North I'll go, the beachless cityless north. The sun has melted into crimson and orange like burgundy wine in neon cheese and below me, over the spires and rooftops, near the cemetery and Carol's complex, the stadium lights spray the sky as if to welcome heavenly messengers. Cankered Mercury leans toward the glow and I see all the streets, all the homes in telescopic detail; parked cars, porch lights coming on, kids involved in after-supper games, lurid deals going down behind flop hotels. I drive faster and the city spins away, the convenience stores and pit stops recede like cars in a plummeting train. I take it to ninety-five, the hood complaining in its casement. I touch the sandalwood and gulp the swampy air through the open window. The car ploughs the susurrations of crickets and cicadas, the croak and moan of raw land pressing the road.

I've never driven this fast.

Already it's starting over. It's turning in, going under, coming up hard and new. I'm a jet-trail in blood-red skies, sheer motion through the original ether. It streams around me, thick and shrill. The car hiccups, the needle wavers.

Oh my soul. My wife.

It spits and loses tach. I guide it onto the shoulder, letting it coast after the engine quits. The floating seconds swell with fate and felt sound, pavement giving way to gravel, hovering between the garish sun and palae-olithic weeds, the distant trees like licks of fire.

For a moment I sit with my hands on the wheel, the world in perfect combustion.

Open the door and step out. Walk around the car and take my jacket and duffel bag from the back seat. Lock the doors. Look up and down the highway, a black and simmering strip through the flaring twilight. The insect din comes in slow, sinister waves.

Walk a few yards beside the asphalt.

When I hear it I turn, thumb out. No remedy this, but final medicine. A van, black as the highway with opaque windows that register the dying sun, dead on and moving fast. Earth around us rises up, hiss and rattle of a thousand tongues.

This is my redeemer, my angel. I know its face.

Here it comes.

Printed in Canada